W9-BVS-766

In July, escape to a world of beautiful locations, glamorous parties and irresistible men—only with Harlequin Presents!

Lucy Monroe brings you a brilliant new story in her ROYAL BRIDES series, *Forbidden: The Billionaire's Virgin Princess,* where Sebastian can't ignore Lina's provocative innocence! Be sure to look out next month for another royal bride! *The Sicilian's Ruthless Marriage Revenge* is the start of Carole Mortimer's sexy new trilogy, THE SICILIANS. Three Sicilians of aristocratic birth seek passion—at any price! And don't miss *The Greek Tycoon's Convenient Wife* by Sharon Kendrick—the fabulous conclusion to her GREEK BILLIONAIRES' BRIDES duet.

Also this month, there are hot desert nights in Penny Jordan's *The Sheikh's Blackmailed Mistress,* a surprise pregnancy in *The Italian's Secret Baby* by Kim Lawrence, a sexy boss in Helen Brooks's *The Billionaire Boss's Secretary Bride* and an incredible Italian in *Under the Italian's Command* by Susan Stephens. Also be sure to read Robyn Grady's fantastic new novel, *The Australian Millionaire's Love-Child!*

We'd love to hear what you think about Presents. E-mail us at Presents@hmb.co.uk or join in the discussions at www.iheartpresents.com and www.sensationalromance.blogspot.com, where you'll also find more information about books and authors!

Dinner at 8

Don't be late!

He's suave and sophisticated.

He's undeniably charming.

And above all, he treats her like a lady....

Beneath the tux, there's a primal, passionate lover who's determined to make her his!

Wined, dined and swept away by a British billionaire!

Helen Brooks

THE BILLIONAIRE BOSS'S SECRETARY BRIDE

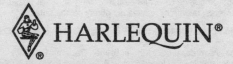

TORONTO • NEW YORK • LONDON
AMSTERDAM • PARIS • SYDNEY • HAMBURG
STOCKHOLM • ATHENS • TOKYO • MILAN • MADRID
PRAGUE • WARSAW • BUDAPEST • AUCKLAND

ISBN-13: 978-0-373-12743-6
ISBN-10:   0-373-12743-X

THE BILLIONAIRE BOSS'S SECRETARY BRIDE

First North American Publication 2008.

www.eHarlequin.com

Printed in U.S.A.

All about the author...
Helen Brooks

HELEN BROOKS was born and educated in
Northampton, England. She met her husband at the age
of sixteeen, and thirty-five years later the magic is still
there. They have three lovely children and a menagerie
of animals in the house! The children, friends and pets
all keep the house buzzing and the food cupboards
empty, but Helen wouldn't have it any other way.

Helen began writing in 1990 as she approached that
milestone of a birthday—forty! She realized her two
teenage ambitions (writing a novel and learning to
drive) had been lost amid babies and family life, so
she set about resurrecting them. Her first novel was
accepted after one rewrite, and she passed her driving
test (the former was a joy and the latter an unmitigated
nightmare).

Helen is a committed Christian and fervent animal
lover. Though she finds time is always at a premium,
she somehow fits in walks in the countryside with
her husband and dogs, meals out followed by the
cinema or theater, reading, swimming and visiting
with friends. She also enjoys sitting in her wonderfully
therapeutic, rambling old garden in the sun with a
glass of red wine (under the guise of resting while
thinking, of course!).

Since becoming a full-time writer, Helen has found
her occupation one of pure joy. She loves exploring
what makes people tick and finds the old adage
"truth is stranger than fiction" to be absolutely true.
She would love to hear from any readers, care of
Harlequin Presents.

CHAPTER ONE

'I STILL can't believe you're really going, that this is your last day. All along I thought you'd change your mind. I mean, you've been here for ever, Gina.'

Gina Leighton couldn't help but smile at her office junior's plaintive voice. 'Perhaps that's why I'm leaving, Natalie,' she said quietly. 'Because I've been here for ever, as you put it.'

OK, so 'for ever' was actually the last eleven years, since she had left university at the age of twenty-one, but clearly as far as Natalie was concerned Gina was as much a part of Breedon & Son as the bricks and mortar. As far as everyone was concerned, most likely. Especially *him*.

'I know I shan't be able to get on with Susan.' Natalie stared at her mournfully. 'She's not like you.'

'You'll be fine,' Gina said bracingly. She didn't mean it. In the last four weeks since she had been showing Susan Richards—her replacement—the ropes, she had come to realise Susan didn't suffer fools gladly. Not that Natalie was a fool, not at all—but she *was* something of a feather-brain at times, who had to have everything explained at least twice for it to click. Susan had already expressed her impatience with the girl in no uncertain terms, ignoring the fact that Natalie was a hard worker and always willing to go the extra mile.

But this wasn't her problem. In a few hours from now, she would walk out of Breedon & Son for the last time. Not only that but she was leaving the Yorkshire market-town where she had been born and raised along with all her friends and family and moving to London at the weekend. New job, new flat, new lifestyle—new everything.

Her stomach doing a fairly good imitation of a pancake on Shrove Tuesday, Gina waved her hand at the papers on her desk. 'I need to finish some things, Natalie, before the drinks and nibbles.' Her boss was putting on a little farewell party for her for the last couple of hours of the afternoon, and she wanted to tie up any loose ends before she left.

Once Natalie had returned to the outer office, however, Gina sat staring round the large and comfortable room that had been her working domain for the last four years, since she had worked her way up to personal secretary to the founder of the agricultural-machinery firm. She'd been thrilled at first, the prestige and extremely generous salary adding to her sense of self-worth. And Dave Breedon was a good boss, a nice family-man with a sense of humour which matched hers. But then Dave Breedon wasn't the reason she was leaving…

'No eleventh-hour change of heart?'

The deep male voice brought Gina's gaze to the doorway. 'Of course not,' she said with a composure that belied her racing heartbeat. But then she had had plenty of practice in disguising how she felt about Harry Breedon, her boss's only son and right-hand man. She stared into the tanned and ruggedly handsome face, her deep blue eyes revealing nothing beyond cool amusement. 'You didn't seriously think there was any chance of that, surely?'

He shrugged. '"Hoped" is perhaps a better word.'

Ridiculous, because she had long since accepted Harry's flirting meant absolutely nothing, but her breathing quickened in spite of herself. 'Sorry,' she said evenly. 'But my bags are already packed.'

'Dad's devastated, you know.' Harry strolled into her office, perching on the edge of her desk and fixing her with smoky grey eyes. Gina tried very hard not to focus on the way his trousers had pulled tight over lean male thighs. And failed.

'Devastated?' she said briskly. 'Hardly. It's nice he'll be sorry to see me go, but I think that's about it, Harry. And Susan is proving to be very capable, as you know.'

Susan Richards. Blonde, attractive and possessed of the sort of figure any model would be grateful for. Just Harry's type, in fact. Over the last twelve months—since Harry had returned to the United Kingdom following his father's heart attack, and taken on more and more of Dave Breedon's work load—Gina had heard the company gossip about his succession of girlfriends, all allegedly blonde and slender. Whereas she was a redhead—at school she'd been called 'carrot top', but she preferred to label her bright auburn locks Titian. And, although her generous hour-glass shape might have been in fashion in Marilyn Monroe's day, it wasn't now.

So why, knowing all that, had she fallen for him? Gina asked herself silently. Especially as he was the original 'love 'em and leave 'em' male. It was the same question she had mulled over umpteen times in the last year, but she was no nearer to a logical answer. But then love didn't pretend to work on logic. All she knew was that this feeling—which had begun with an earthy lust that had knocked her sideways, and had rapidly grown into a love that was all consuming the more she'd got to know him—was here to stay. Whereas to Harry she was merely the secretary he shared with his father—admittedly someone he liked to chat and laugh and flirt with, but then he'd be the same with any female. End of story.

'I didn't think you liked London when you were at uni there. I remember you saying you couldn't wait to get home.'

Gina frowned. 'I said I was *glad* to come home.' She corrected quietly. 'That didn't mean I didn't like the city.'

He stared at her for a moment before hitching himself off her desk and standing to his feet. 'Well, it's your life,' he said so reasonably Gina wanted to hit him. 'I just hope you don't regret it, that's all. All big cities can be lonely places.'

'The old thing about being surrounded by people but knowing no one?' Gina nodded. 'I've lots of old university friends living in London, so that's not a problem. And I'm sharing a flat with another girl, anyway. I'm not living alone.'

She didn't add she was feeling more than a little trepidation about that. For the last six years she'd had her own place, a small but beautifully positioned top-floor flat in a big house on the edge of town, with views of the river. After living with her parents, she had revelled in having a home of her own, where she was answerable to no one and could please herself at weekends, getting up when she wanted and eating when she felt like it. But renting in London was vastly different from renting in Yorkshire, and although her new job paid very well she couldn't run to her own place.

'Don't forget to leave your new address.' He was already walking to the door. 'I might look you up next time I spend a few days in the capital. Doss down on your sofa for a night.'

Over her dead body. She took a deep breath and let it out evenly. 'Fine,' she said nonchalantly, wishing she could hate him. It would make everything so much easier—she wouldn't be uprooting herself for one thing. Although, no, that wasn't quite fair. Even before she'd fallen for Harry she'd acknowledged she was in a rut and needed to do something with her life. Both her sisters and most of her friends were married with children; going out with them wasn't what it had once been. In the twelve months before Harry had come on the scene, she'd only had the odd date or two, as the only men around had either been boring or convinced they were God's gift to women, or, worse, married and looking for a bit of fun on the side. She'd begun to see herself as a spinster: devoted to her job, her home, and godmother to other people's children.

Her friends thought she was too choosy. She stared at the door Harry had just closed behind him. And maybe she was. Certainly she'd had offers, but she balked at the idea of *trying* to like someone. Either the spark was there or it wasn't. Besides which, she wasn't desperate to settle down. What she *was* desperate for was a life outside work that was interesting and exciting and carried a buzz—nightclubs, the theatre, good restaurants and good company. She was only thirty two, for goodness' sake! So London had beckoned, and she'd embraced the notion.

It was the right decision. She nodded at the thought. Definitely. Without a doubt. Of course, if Harry had shown any interest…But he hadn't. And so roses round the door, cosy log-fires and breakfast in bed for two with the Sunday papers wasn't an option.

Gina swallowed the lump in her throat, telling herself she'd cried enough tears over him. However hard it was going to be to say goodbye, it would have been emotional suicide to stay. That one brief kiss at Christmas had told her that. Merely a friendly peck on her cheek as far as he was concerned, when he'd wished her merry Christmas. But the feel of his lips, the closeness of him, the delicious smell of his aftershave, had sent her into a spin for hours.

Christmas had been a bitter-sweet affair, and it was then she'd decided enough was enough. Self-torture wasn't her style. And it had been added confirmation when on the afternoon of Boxing Day, whilst she'd been walking her parents' dogs in the snowy fields surrounding the town, she'd seen him in the distance with the blonde of the moment. She had hidden behind a tree and prayed they wouldn't see her, but once the danger was over and she'd continued her walk she'd realised merely leaving Breedon & Son wasn't enough. She had to get right away, where there was no chance of running into him.

And now it was the beginning of April. D-Day. Outside spring had come with a vengeance the last few days, croci and daffodils bursting forth, and birds busy nesting—new life sprouting seemingly everywhere. And that was the way she had to look at this, as an opportunity for new life. No point feeling her world had come to an end, no point at all.

Nevertheless, it was with gritted teeth that she joined everyone in the work canteen later that afternoon. She was touched to see most of Breedon & Son's employees—over a hundred in all, counting the folk on the factory floor—had gathered to say goodbye, and even more overcome when she was given a satellite-navigation system for her car to which everyone had contributed.

'So you can find your way back to us now and again,' Bill Dent, the chief accountant, joked as he presented her with the gift. She had a reputation—richly deserved—of having no sense of direction or navigation skills, and over the last weeks had endured a host of teasing about negotiating city streets.

'Thank you all so much.' As she gave a tearful little speech she kept her gaze from focusing on one tall, dark figure standing a little apart from the rest of the throng, but she was still vitally aware of every movement Harry made. She knew exactly when Susan Richards made her way over to him, for instance, and the way the other woman reached up on tiptoe to whisper something in his ear.

All in all, Gina was glad when after an hour or so people began to drift home. Loving someone who didn't love you was bad enough at the best of times, but when you were trying to be bright and cheerful, and keep a lid on a mounting volcano of tears, it didn't help to see the object of your desire receiving the full batting-eyelash treatment from an undeniably attractive blonde.

When there was just a handful of people left, Gina made her way back to her office to pick up the last of her things. She felt like a wet rag. Dropping into her chair, she glanced round the room, feeling unbearably sentimental.

Dave entered a moment later, Harry on his heels. Shaking his head, Dave said, 'Don't look like that. I told you, you shouldn't leave us. Everyone thinks the world of you.'

Not everyone. Forcing a smile, Gina managed to keep her voice light and even as she said, 'The big wide world beckons, and it's now or never. It was always going to be hard to say goodbye.'

'While we're on that subject...' Dave reached into his pocket and brought out a small, oblong gift-wrapped box. 'This is a personal thank-you, lass. I'm not buttering you up when I say you've been the best secretary I've ever had. It's the truth. If London isn't all it's cracked up to be, there'll always be a job somewhere in Breedon & Son for you.'

'Oh, it's beautiful.' After unwrapping the gift, Gina gazed, entranced, at the delicate little gold watch the box held. 'Thank you so much. I didn't expect…' The lump in her throat prevented further speech.

'Harry chose it,' said Dave, looking uncomfortable at the show of emotion. He was all down to earth, blunt Yorkshireman, and prided himself on it. 'I was going to give you a cheque, more practical in my opinion, but he thought you'd like something to remind you of your time here, and he noticed you hadn't been wearing your watch the last few weeks.'

'It broke,' she whispered. *He had noticed.*

'Aye, well, there we are, then.' Dave clearly wanted to end what was to him an embarrassing few moments. 'Don't forget to look us up when you're back visiting your parents. All right, lass? I'll be off now, the missus and I are out for dinner tonight. Lock up the offices, would you, Harry?' he added, turning to his son. 'The factory's already been taken care of.'

'Goodbye, Mr Breedon.' Gina stood up to shake her boss's hand—he was of the old school, and didn't hold with social pleasantries such as kissing or hugging—but then on impulse quickly pressed her lips to the leathery old cheek before she sat down again.

Dave cleared his throat. 'Bye, lass. You look after yourself,' he said gruffly before disappearing out of the door.

Silence reigned for some moments while Gina tidied the last few papers on her desk. Every nerve and muscle was screaming, and the blood was racing through her veins. *Act cool. Keep calm and businesslike. Don't give yourself away. You knew this moment was going to come.*

Yes, she answered the voice in her head. But she hadn't expected they would be alone when she had to say the final goodbye.

'Your car wasn't in its normal spot in the car park this morning.'

Surprised, Gina raised her head, and looked fully at him for the first time since he'd entered the room. He gazed back at her from where he was leaning against the wall, hands in the pockets of his trousers and grey eyes half-closed, their expression inscrutable. She'd noticed this ability to betray nothing of what he was thinking early on. It was probably part and parcel of what had made him so successful in his own right since leaving university and working abroad, first in Germany and Austria, and then in the States. By all accounts he had left an extremely well paid and powerful position in a massive chain of pharmaceutical companies in America when he had returned to help his father, although she had learned this from Dave Breedon. Harry never talked about his past, and when she had asked the odd question his replies had been monosyllabic.

'My car?' She tried to collect her thoughts. It was difficult with him looking so broodingly drop-dead gorgeous. 'I knew I'd be having a drink, so I decided to travel by taxi today.' It was only partly the truth. She hadn't known how she would feel when the knowledge that she would never see him again became reality.

'No need.' He straightened, and her stomach muscles clenched. 'I'll run you home.'

No, no, no. She had seen his car, a sexy sports job that moved like greased lightning, and it was seduction on wheels. 'Thanks, but that's not necessary. It's the wrong direction for you.'

He smiled. She wondered if he knew what a devastating effect it had on the opposite sex. Probably, she thought a trifle maliciously.

'It's a beautiful spring evening, and I'm not doing anything. I've all the time in the world,' he drawled lazily.

'No, really, I'd feel awful putting you to so much trouble.'

'I insist.' He brushed aside the desperate refusal.

'And I insist on travelling by taxi.' She could be just as determined as him. The thought that she might suffer the unthinkable humiliation of giving herself away necessitated it.

'Don't be silly.' He walked over and perched on her desk— a habit of his—lifting her chin and looking into her eyes as he said softly, 'You're all upset at leaving, and no wonder. You've been here since the beginning of time. I can't possibly abandon you to the anonymity of a taxi.'

She didn't like the 'beginning of time' bit. Who did he think she was—Methuselah? And she despised herself for the way her whole insides had tightened at his touch. But they always did, however casual the action. 'You're not abandoning me,' she said stiffly. 'It's my choice.'

'A bad one.' He slid off the desk and walked to the door, opening it before he turned and said, 'And therefore I'm fully justified in overruling it. I'll get my coat.'

'Harry!' she shouted as he went to disappear.

'Yes, Gina?' He popped his head back round the door, grinning.

She gave up. 'This is ridiculous,' she muttered ungraciously. And dangerous. For her.

'Put your coat on and stop grumbling.'

He was back within a minute or so, taking the satellite-navigation system from her as she met him in the outer office. 'You'd better have my keys.' She handed him her office keys, which included those to all the confidential files. 'I meant to give them to Susan earlier.' *But she was so busy making goo-goo eyes at you I never got the chance.*

He pocketed them without comment.

She had slipped the case holding the watch into her handbag, and as they walked towards the lift she said quietly, 'Thank you for thinking of the watch, Harry. It's really beautiful.'

'My pleasure.' Once inside the carpet-lined box, he added, 'Dad really meant what he said, you know, and the watch is from both of us. You were great when he had his heart attack, holding the fort here, and then putting in endless hours once I was having to pick up all the threads. I couldn't have done it without you, Gina.'

This was torture. Exquisite torture, perhaps, but torture nonetheless. 'Anyone would have done the same.'

'No, they wouldn't.' His voice deepened, taking on the smoky quality that was dynamite as he murmured, 'I just wanted to say thank you.'

The lift easily carried twelve people, but suddenly it was much too small. She caught the faintest whiff of his aftershave and breathed it in greedily. Drawing on all her considerable willpower, she said evenly, 'There's no need, I was just doing my job, but it's nice to know I'm appreciated.' She forced a smile as the lift doors opened, stepping into the small reception with a silent sigh of relief. Too cosy. Too intimate. And the car was going to be as bad.

It was worse. Every single nerve in her body registered the impact as, after settling her in the passenger seat and shutting the door, Harry joined her in the car. The interior was all black leather with a state-of-the-art dashboard, but it was the close confines of the car that had Gina swallowing hard. Her voice something of a squeak, she said, 'This is a lovely car.' Understatement of the year. 'Toys for boys?' she added, attempting a wry smile.

He turned his head, smiling. He was so close she could see every little, black hair of his five o'clock stubble in spite of the gathering twilight. 'I had one of these in the States, and I guess I got used to fast cars.'

And fast women, no doubt. Not that any of his girlfriends lasted for more than five minutes. Gina nodded. 'It must have been a wrench to leave America.'

'Yes, it was.' He started the engine before turning to her again. 'How about dinner?'

'What?' She stared at him, utterly taken aback.

'Dinner?' he repeated patiently. 'Unless you've other plans? I thought it might be a nice way to round off your time at Breedon & Son. A small thank-you.'

'You've already thanked me with the watch,' she said, flustered beyond measure, and hoping he wouldn't notice.

'That was a combined thank-you. This is just me.'

Whatever he was, he wasn't 'just' anything. And it would be crazy to say yes. The whole evening would be spent trying to hide her feelings and play at being friendly, when just looking at him made her weak at the knees. But she would never have the chance of another evening of his company, that was for sure. Two more days of tying up all the loose ends, and she was off to London for good. Could she cope with the agony of being with him? It would mess her head up for days.

'My other plans were clearing out cupboards and beginning to spring-clean the flat,' she admitted weakly. 'It can wait.'

'Good. Dinner it is, then. There's a great little Italian place not far from where I live. Do you like Italian food?'

She didn't think she would taste a thing tonight anyway. 'I love it.'

'I'll make sure they've got a table.' He extracted his mobile phone, punching in a number before saying, 'Roberto?' and then speaking in rapid Italian. She hadn't known he could speak the language, but it didn't particularly surprise her. That was Harry all over. 'That's settled.' He smiled at her. 'Eight o'clock. OK with you if we call at my place first? I'd like to put on a fresh shirt before we go.'

His place. She'd see where he lived. She'd be able to picture him there in the weeks and months to follow. Not a good idea, probably, but irresistibly tempting. 'Fine,' she nodded, drawing on the cool aplomb she'd developed over the last twelve months, as the powerful car leapt into life and left the car park far too fast.

She glanced at Harry's hands on the steering wheel. Large, capable, masculine hands. What would it feel like to have them move over every inch of her body, explore her intimate places, along with his mouth and tongue? To savour and taste…

'…parents now and again.'

'Sorry?' Too late she realised he'd spoken, but she had been deep in a shockingly erotic fantasy. Blushing scarlet—an unfortunate attribute which went with the hair and her pale, freckled skin—she lied, 'I was thinking how nice everyone's been today.'

'Of course they've been nice. You're very popular.'

She didn't want to be popular. She wanted to be a slender,

elegant siren with long blonde hair and come-to-bed eyes, the sort of woman who might capture his heart, given half a chance.

'I was just saying we must keep in touch, and perhaps meet up for lunch now and again when you visit your parents,' he continued easily. 'I count you as a friend, Gina. I hope you know that.'

Great. 'As I do you.' She smiled brightly. Once she was in London, he'd forget she'd ever existed within days. Probably by the time he got up tomorrow morning, in fact. Harry wasn't the sort of man who had women *friends*. Just *women*.

The cool spring twilight had almost completely given way to the shadows of night by the time Harry turned the car off the country lane they had been following for some time, and through open wrought-iron gates on to a scrunchy pebble drive. Gina was surprised how far they'd travelled; she hadn't realised his home was so far away from Breedon & Son. She had supposed he'd settled somewhere near his parents' home.

The drive wound briefly between mature evergreens and bushes, which effectively hid all sight of the building from the road, and then suddenly became bordered by a wide expanse of green lawn with the house in front of them. Gina hadn't known what to expect. Probably a no-nonsense modern place or elegant turn-of-the-century manor-type house. In the event the picturesque thatched cottage in front of her was neither of these.

'This is your home?'

She had asked the obvious, but he didn't appear to notice. 'Like it?' he asked casually as the car drew up on the horseshoe-shaped area in front of the cottage.

Did she like it? How could anyone fail to? The two-storey cottage's white walls and traditional mullioned windows were topped by a high thatched roof out of which peeped gothick dormers. The roof overhung to form an encircling veranda, supported on ancient, gnarled tree-trunks on which a table and chairs sat ready for summer evenings. There was even evidence of roses round the door on the trellis bordering the quaint arched door, and red and green ivy covered the walls of the veranda. It was so quintessentially the perfect English country-cottage that Gina was speechless. It was the last place, the *very* last place, she would have expected Harry to buy, and definitely no bachelor pad.

Whether he guessed what she was thinking or her face had given her away Gina wasn't sure, but the next moment he drawled, 'I had a modern stainless-steel and space-age place in the States, overlooking the ocean; I fancied a change.'

'It's wonderful.' He opened the car door as he spoke, and now as he appeared at her side and helped her out of the passenger seat she repeated, 'It's wonderful. A real fairy-tale cottage. I half expect Goldilocks and the three bears to appear any moment.' She liked that. It was light, teasing. She'd got the fleeting impression he hadn't appreciated her amazement at his choice of home, despite his lazy air.

He shrugged. 'It's somewhere to lay my hat for the moment. I'm not into putting down roots.'

She'd been right. He *hadn't* wanted her to assume there was any danger of him becoming a family man in the future. Not that she would. 'Hence your travelling in the past?' she said carefully as they walked to the front door.

'I guess.'

She stared at him. 'Your father's hoping you'll take over the family business at some point, isn't he?'

'That was never on the cards.' He opened the door, standing aside so she preceded him into the wide square hall. The old floorboards had been lovingly restored and varnished, their mellow tones reflected in the honey-coloured walls adorned with the odd print or two. 'I agreed to come and help my father over the next couple of years, partly to ease him into letting go of the strings and making it easier to sell when the time comes, but that's all.'

'I see.' She didn't, but it was none of her business. 'So, you'll go back to the States at some point?'

Again he shrugged. 'The States, Germany, perhaps even Australia. I'm not sure. I invested a good deal of the money I've earned over the last years, played the stock exchange and so on. I don't actually need to work, but I will. I like a challenge.'

It was the most he had ever said about himself, and Gina longed to ask more, but a closed look had come over his face. Changing the subject, she said, 'Everything looks extremely clean and dust free. Do you have a cleaner come in?'

'Are you saying men can't clean for themselves? That's a trifle sexist, isn't it?' He grinned at her, leading the way to what proved to be the sitting room, and he opened the door into a large room dominated by a magnificent open fireplace, the wooden floors scattered with fine rugs, and the sofas and chairs soft and plumpy. 'You're right, though,' he admitted unrepentantly. 'Mrs Rothman comes in three days a week, and does everything from changing the lightbulbs to washing and ironing. She's a treasure.'

'And preparing your meals?' she asked as he waved her to a seat.

'Not at all. I'm a great cook, if I do say so myself, and I prefer to eat what I want when I want to eat it. Glass of wine while you wait?' he added. 'Red or white?'

'Red, please.' She glanced at the fireplace as he disappeared, presumably to the kitchen. There were the remains of a fire in the fireplace, and plenty of logs were stacked in the ample confines of the hearth. She pictured him sitting here in the evenings, sipping a glass of wine maybe, while he stared into the flickering flames. The wrench her heart gave warned her to keep her thoughts in check. And she wasn't going to dwell on the likelihood of the blonde of the moment stretched out on a rug in front of the fire, either, with Harry pampering and pleasing her.

'One glass of wine.'

Gina was brought out of her mental agony as Harry reappeared, an enormous half-full glass of deep-red wine in one hand. She took it with a doubtful smile. There must have been half a bottle in there, and she'd been too het up to eat any of the extensive nibbles earlier, or much lunch, for that matter.

'I won't be long. There's some magazines there—' he gestured towards one of the occasional tables dotted about the room '—and some nuts and olives alongside them. Help yourself.'

'Thank you.' As soon as he'd left again, she scuttled across and made short work of half the bowl of nuts, deciding she'd worry about the calories tomorrow. Tonight she needed to be sober and in full charge of her senses. One slip, one look, and he might guess how she felt about him, and then she'd die. She would, she'd die. Or have to go on living with the knowledge she'd betrayed herself, and that would be worse.

She retrieved her glass of wine and sipped at it as she wandered about the room. Rich, dark and fruity, it was gorgeous. Like Harry. Although he had never been fruity with her, more was the pity.

She glanced at herself in the huge antique mirror over the

fireplace. The mellow lighting in the room made her hair appear more golden than anything else, and blended the pale ginger freckles that covered her creamy skin from head to foot into an overall honey glow. It couldn't do anything for her small snub nose and nondescript features, however. She frowned at her reflection, her blue eyes dark with irritation. This was the reason Harry had never come on to her. She was the epitome of the girl next door, when she longed to be a *femme fatale:* tall, slim, elegant—not busty and hippy. Even her mother had to admit she was 'nicely rounded', which meant—in the terms the rest of the world would use—she was on the plump side.

After staring at herself for a full minute, she walked over to the window and looked out over the grounds at the back of the cottage while she finished her glass of wine. She needed something to give her dutch courage for the evening, considering Harry was accompanying a creature not far removed from the Hunchback of Nôtre Dame.

'You can't see much tonight.'

He must have crept into the room, because she hadn't heard him coming. Gina was glad there was no wine in the glass, because with the jump she gave as he came up behind her it would have been all down her dress. He continued to stand behind her, his hands loosely on her waist, as he said, 'To the left beyond that big chestnut tree there's a swimming pool, but it's too dark to see it, and a tennis court. Are you sporty?'

Sporty? She didn't know what she was with him holding her like this. Dredging up what was left of her thought process, she managed to mumble, 'I swim a bit.' She didn't add that she hadn't played tennis for years, because whatever sports bra she bought it still didn't seem to stop her breasts bobbing about like crazy. Too much information, for sure.

'You'll have to come and have a swim in the summer, if you're up this neck of the woods.'

That *so* wasn't an option. 'That'd be great.'

'If you're ready, we'll make a move.'

When he let go of her, she felt wildly relieved and hopelessly bereft. When she turned to face him it didn't help her shaky equilibrium one bit. He'd obviously had a quick shower along with changing, and his ebony hair was still damp and slightly tousled. Suddenly he appeared vastly different from the immaculately finished product during working hours, and the open-necked black shirt and casual black trousers he was wearing added to the transformation. In the designer suits, shirts and ties he favoured in the office, he was breathtakingly gorgeous. Now he was a walking sex-machine, with enough magnetism to cause a disturbance in the earth's orbit.

Controlling a rush of love so powerful she was amazed it didn't show, Gina handed him her empty glass and walked over to the sofa, where her handbag and jacket were, saying over her shoulder, 'This is very good of you, Harry. There was nothing more exciting than beans on toast waiting for me at the flat.'

'My pleasure.'

No, hers, given the merest encouragement, Gina thought wryly. She had never been tempted to go all the way with any of her boyfriends in the past, and had even begun to wonder if there was something wrong with her. Harry's entrance into her life had put paid to that. She only had to think about him to get embarrassingly aroused. If he ever actually made love to her...

He took her jacket from her, helping her into it with a warm smile. She was everlastingly thankful he couldn't read her mind. Taking a deep breath, she walked briskly out of the room.

CHAPTER TWO

WHY had he done this? Why had he invited her out to dinner tonight? He hadn't intended to. He'd meant their goodbye to be friendly, swift and final, and definitely with a third party present.

As Harry slid into the car, he glanced at Gina for a second. He was, by virtue of his genetic background and upbringing, a very rational man. 'Cold' had even been the word used by former girlfriends on occasion, but that had been after he had firmly disabused them of the idea that their relationship had any chance of becoming permanent.

He knew exactly what he wanted out of life. Since Anna. And, because the knowledge had been forged in the furnace, it was not negotiable—Independence. Following his own star, with no tentacles of responsibility to prevent him doing so. Companionship and sex along the way, of course, good times with women who knew the score. But nothing that came with strings and ties and required sacrifices he wasn't willing to make.

He'd left university with a first in business studies, gaining experience in a couple of jobs, before landing the big one in the States where he'd moved to the top of the ladder after acquiring a postgraduate degree, Master of Business Administration. He had enjoyed working for that, although with his job it had meant regular twenty-hour days. But that had been fine. It had happened after Anna, and anything which had enabled him to go to bed too dog-tired to think had been OK by him.

'Is it far?'

The soft voice at the side of him brought his head turning. 'Just a couple of miles,' he said evenly, swinging the car out of the drive onto the quiet tree-lined lane beyond. 'It's only a very small place, by the way, nothing grand, but the food is excellent. Roberto has the knack of turning the most simple dish into something special. The first time I saw a warm-bread salad with roasted red peppers on the menu, I thought it a fairly basic starter. Big mistake. It came with capers and anchovies and fresh basil, and a whole host of other ingredients, that made it out of this world.'

'You're making my mouth water.'

Harry smiled. 'Do I take it you're someone who lives to eat, rather than eats to live?'

His swift glance saw her wrinkle her little nose. 'Can't you tell?' she said a trifle flatly.

His smile vanished. He didn't know what it was about this gentle, ginger-haired woman that had attracted him from day one, but her softly rounded, somewhat voluptuous curves were part of it. 'Your figure's fine,' he said firmly.

'Thank you.'

'I mean it. There are far too many women these days who don't actually *look* like women. Lettuce leaves are great for rabbits, but there's where they should stop. I hate to see a woman nibbling on a stick of celery all evening, and drinking mineral water, while insisting she's full to bursting.'

He'd just pulled up before turning on to the main road, and

in the shadowed confines of the car he caught her glance of disbelief. 'What?' he said, turning to face her.

'You might say that, but I bet the women you date are all stick insects.'

He opened his mouth to deny it before the uncomfortable truth hit. To anyone on the outside looking in, it would appear Gina was spot-on-target. He *did* tend to date trim, svelte types. Why? He pulled on to the main road, his very able and intelligent mind dissecting the matter.

Because he'd found by experience that women who were obsessed with their figures, and appearance, and street cred, tended to be on the insular side—especially when they were also career minded, as he made sure all his girlfriends were. Less inclined towards cosy twosomes at home, and more likely to favour a date involving dinner and dancing, or the theatre, where they could see and be seen. Women with their own, forged-in-steel goals who weren't looking for happy-ever-after but good conversation, good company and entertainment, and good sex. He'd made the odd mistake, of course, but mostly he tended to get it right.

In fact, if he thought about it, one criterion for dating a woman more than a couple of times was her level of self-interest. He grimaced mentally. Which made him…what? He decided not to follow that train of thought, but it confirmed he'd been crazy to take Gina out tonight, even on the basis of friendship.

Realising he hadn't given her any reply, he ducked the issue by saying self-righteously, 'Anorexia is becoming an ever-increasing problem these days, and no one in their right mind can say those women, young girls some of them, look attractive.'

'I suppose not.'

They drove in silence for the rest of the short journey. When he finally pulled into Roberto's tiny car-park, he saw Gina looking about her. The restaurant was situated on the edge of a typical Yorkshire market-town, but in the darkness it appeared more secluded than it was. In the muted lighting from the couple of lamps in the car park, her hair gleamed like strands of copper. He wondered what she would say if he asked her to loosen it from the upswept bun she usually favoured for work. He'd seen it down a couple of times, and it was beautiful.

Stupid. He brushed the notion away ruthlessly. This was dinner. Nothing else.

He slid out of the car, walking round the bonnet and then opening Gina's door and helping her out. The air smelt of the burgeoning vegetation, and somewhere close by a blackbird sang two or three flute-like notes—probably disturbed by the car and lights—before falling silent again. He watched as she drew in a lungful of air, her eyes closed. Opening them, she said softly. 'I shall miss this in London.'

'Don't go, then.' He hadn't meant to say it.

'I have to.' Her lashes flickered.

'Why?'

'I start my new job on Monday—I've got a flat, everything. I couldn't let people down.'

He suddenly knew why he had asked her out to dinner. He hadn't believed she would actually leave Breedon & Son when it came to the crunch. He hadn't prepared himself for her disappearing out of his life. There had been so much talk among Natalie and the other employees of Gina changing her mind at the last minute, and he'd found it expedient to believe it. He should have known that once she had committed to something she wouldn't turn back.

'No, I guess you couldn't.' At six feet, he topped her by five or six inches, and as he gazed down at her he caught the scent of her perfume, something warm and silky that reminded him of magnolia flowers. The jump his senses gave provided a warning shot across the bows. 'Let's go in,' he said coolly. 'I'm starving.'

Once Roberto had finished fussing over them, and they were seated at a table for two with menus in front of them and a bottle of wine on order, Harry took himself in hand. This was her last day at Breedon & Son, and it was true that she had been a lifesaver when he'd returned so suddenly to the UK—*that* was why he'd offered to take her out tonight. Nothing else. And of course he'd miss her. You couldn't work closely with someone umpteen hours a day, share the odd coffee break and lunch and learn about her life and so on, without missing her when she was gone. It was as simple as that.

'I think I'm going to try that warm-bread salad you mentioned for starters.' She stared at him, her blue eyes dark in the paleness of her skin. 'And maybe the tagliatelle to follow?'

'Good choice.' He nodded. 'I'll join you.'

Once Roberto had returned with the wine and taken their order, he settled back in his seat and raised his glass in a toast. 'To you and your new life in the great, big city,' he said, purposely injecting a teasing note into his voice. 'May you be protected from all the prowling wolves who might try to gobble you up.'

She laughed. 'I don't somehow think they'll be queueing for the privilege.'

He'd noticed this before, her tendency towards self-deprecation. 'From where I'm sitting, it's a very real possibility,' he said quietly.

Her voice a little uncertain, she said, 'Thank you. You're very gallant.'

'I like to think so, but in this case I am speaking the truth.' He leant forward slightly, not hiding his curiosity as he said, 'You don't rate yourself much, do you, Gina? Why is that— or is that too personal a question?'

He liked it that she could blush. He'd thought it a lost art before he had met her.

She shrugged. 'Legacy of being the ugly duckling of the family, I suppose,' she said quietly. 'My two older sisters inherited the red hair, but theirs is true chestnut, and they don't have freckles. Added to which it was me who had to have the brace on my teeth and see a doctor about acne.'

His eyes wandered over the flawlessly creamy skin, flawless except for the freckles, but he liked those. And her teeth were small, white and even. 'Your dentist and doctor are to be congratulated on their part in assisting the swan to emerge. You're a very lovely woman, even if you don't realise it.'

The blush grew deeper. He watched it with fascination. When she looked ready to explode, he said, 'I seem to remember both your sisters are married, aren't they?' It was more to change the subject and alleviate her distress than because he cared two hoots about them.

She nodded, and her hair reflected a hundred different shades of gold and copper as she moved. 'Bryony has a little boy of three, and Margaret two girls of five and eight, so I'm an aunt three times over. They're all great kids.'

Something in her voice prompted him to say, 'You obviously are very fond of them.'

'Of course.'

There was no 'of course' about it. He knew several women who couldn't seem to stand their own children, let alone anyone else's. 'Do you see yourself settling down and having a family one day?'

A shadow passed over her face. 'Maybe.'

'Maybe?'

She smiled, but he could see it was a little shaky. Her mouth was soft, vulnerable. Muscles knotted in his stomach.

'Settling down and having a family does carry the pre-requisite of meeting the right man,' she said, taking a sip of her wine.

'You're bound to meet someone in London.'

'Why "bound to"?'

Her voice was sharper than he'd heard it before, and his eyes widened momentarily. He'd clearly said the wrong thing, although he couldn't think how.

And then she said quickly, 'Not everyone meets the right one, as I'm sure you'd agree, and personally I'd rather remain single than marry just to be with someone. I'm going to London with a view to furthering my career, and perhaps travelling a little, things like that.'

He stared at her. That wasn't all of it. Had she had a love affair go wrong? Was she moving away because someone had hurt her, broken her heart? But she hadn't said anything to him about a man in her life.

He caught at the feeling of anger, the sense that she had let him down in some way. Drawing on his considerable self-control, he said coolly, 'I hadn't got you down as a career woman, Gina?'

'No?' She glanced up from her wine glass and looked him

full in the face, but he could read nothing from her expression when she said, 'But then you don't really know me, do you?'

He felt as though she had just slapped him round the face, even though her voice had been pleasant and calm. He thought he knew her. She had always been quite free in talking about herself, her family, her friends, although… His eyes narrowed. Come to think of it, she had never discussed her love life at all. He'd just assumed she didn't have one, he supposed.

He felt a dart of self-disgust, and realised how much he had assumed. Trying to justify himself, he argued silently, no, it wasn't altogether that. Because he didn't like to talk about that side of his life, he hadn't pressed her in that direction, that was all.

And the long hours she had put in ever since he had arrived? The devotion to the job, and to him and his father? Her readiness to be prepared to work overtime at the drop of a hat? The way—even when her workload had been huge and she'd been working flat out—she'd spare time to talk him through a procedure he wasn't familiar with? He had taken it all for granted, looking back, in his arrogance having imagined Breedon & Son was all of her life. But why would it be? Looking like Gina did, why wouldn't there have been a man in the background somewhere?

Collecting his racing thoughts, he said, 'So, what's your ultimate goal? Do you intend to stay in the capital for good, now you've made the break?'

She paused to think. He saw her tongue stroke her bottom lip for a moment, and his body responded, stirring to life. 'I'm not sure.' She raised her eyes. 'Possibly. Like I said, I'd like to travel, and perhaps that could be incorporated into a job. That would be perfect.'

This was a new side to her. *Disturbing*. He'd been more than a little taken aback when she had announced her intention to leave shortly after the New Year; it hadn't fitted into his overall picture of her. She was level-headed, reliable, a calm, balanced woman with both feet firmly on the ground. The very last person to suddenly announce they were leaving their home, job and friends to hightail it to the big city, in fact.

'I see.' He tried for nonchalance when he said, 'You're full of surprises, Gina Leighton. I had you down as more of a homebody, I guess. Someone who wouldn't be happy if they were far away from where they were born.'

'London isn't exactly the ends of the earth.'

She lifted her chin as she spoke, and he said quickly, 'Oh, don't get me wrong. That wasn't a criticism.'

'Good.' She sipped at her wine.

'If anyone can understand the urge to travel, I can. It's just that I saw you differently, more…'

'Boring?'

'Boring?' He stared at her in genuine amazement. 'Of course I never thought you were boring. How can you say that? I was going to say contented with what you had, where you were in life.'

'You can be all that and still fancy a change,' she said flatly, just as the waitress came with their warm-bread salads.

Once she'd gone, he reached across the table and touched Gina's hand for one brief moment. 'I didn't mean to offend you,' he said softly. 'And I swear I've never thought of you as boring.' Disconcerting, maybe. Definitely unsettling on occasion, like when he'd stolen a swift kiss at the Christmas party and the scent of her had stayed with him all evening. And, on the couple of instances she'd worn her hair down for work, he'd had to stuff his hands in his pockets all day to avoid the temptation to take a handful of the shining, silky mass and nuzzle his face into it. But boring? Never.

Gina shrugged. 'It doesn't matter one way or the other.'

She had moved her fingers out from under his almost as soon as they had rested on her hand, and it suggested she was still annoyed.

'It does.' Irritated, his voice hardened. 'We're friends, aren't we?'

'We are—we were—work colleagues, first and foremost,' came the dampening answer. 'We were *friendly,* but that's not the same as being friends.'

He stared at her. Her cheeks were flushed and her eyes were bright, and he couldn't read a thing in her closed expression. He couldn't remember the last time he had felt out of his depth when speaking to a woman, but it was happening now. Raking back a lock of hair from his forehead, he leant back in his seat, surveying her broodingly. 'So, what's your definition of friends?'

She ate a morsel of bread and pronounced it delicious, before she said, 'Friends are there for you, right or wrong. You can have fun with them or cry with them. They know plenty about you, but stick in there with you nonetheless. They're part of your life.'

He became aware he was frowning, and straightened his face. He felt monumentally insulted. 'And none of that applies to us, apparently? Is that what you're saying?' he said evenly.

'Well, does it?' she asked matter-of-factly.

'I think so.'

'Harry, we've never met out of work, and know very little about each other.'

He shook his head stubbornly. 'Don't be silly, we know plenty about each other,' he said firmly, his annoyance rising when she narrowed her eyes cynically. He was possessed by the very irrational desire to do or say something remarkable to shock her out of her complacency, something that hadn't happened since he had been a thirteen-year-old schoolboy trying to impress the school beauty. But Delia Sherwood had been a walkover compared to the self-contained, quiet young woman watching him with disbelieving eyes. And this was a crazy conversation. He wasn't even sure how it had come about. Why did Gina's opinion about their relationship matter so much, anyway? 'I know you have two sisters, a best friend called Erica, and that you walk your parents' dog to keep fit, for instance. OK?' Even to himself he sounded petulant.

'Those are head facts. Not *heart* facts.'

'I'm sorry?' he said, his temper rising.

She gave what sounded like a weary sigh and ate another mouthful of food. 'Think about it,' was all she said.

He ate his warm-bread salad without tasting it. There had been undercurrents in their friendship from day one—and it was a friendship, whatever she said—but there she was, as cool as a cucumber, stating they were merely work colleagues. Damn it, he *knew* there was a spark there, even if neither of them had done anything about it. And the reason he'd held his hand had been for *her* sake. An act of consideration on his part.

He speared a piece of pepper with unnecessary violence, feeling extremely hard done by. He had known she wasn't the type of woman to have a meaningless affair, and because he couldn't offer anything permanent he'd kept things light and casual. But that didn't mean there wasn't something real between them.

The waitress appeared as soon as they had finished and whisked their plates away, whereupon Gina immediately stood up, reaching for her handbag as she did so. 'I'm just going to powder my nose,' she said brightly.

He had risen to his feet and now he nodded, sitting down again, watching her make her way to the back of the small restaurant and open the door marked *Ladies*.

He had thought he knew her, but she had proved him wrong. His frown deepened. The woman who had sat there and blatantly told him he could stick their friendship—or as good as—was not the Gina of nine-to-five. In fact, she was a stranger. A beautiful, soft, honey-skinned stranger, admittedly, with eyes that could be uncertain and vulnerable one moment and fiery, to match the hair—the next. But a stranger nonetheless. And he didn't understand it.

Harry finished his glass of wine but resisted pouring himself another as he was driving, instead reaching for the bottle of sparkling mineral-water he'd ordered along with the wine.

He had imagined there was a…buzz between them, and all the time she'd probably been carrying on with someone else. Of course she'd been entitled to; he'd had one or two, maybe three—but very short-lived—relationships in the last twelve months. But it was different for her. And then he grimaced at the hypocrisy, scowling in self-contempt. Damn it, she'd caught him on the raw, and he didn't know which end of him was up. Which only confirmed a million times over he had been absolutely right not to get involved with Gina. She was trouble. In spite of the air of gentle, warm voluptuousness that had a man dreaming he could drown in the depths of her—or perhaps *because* of it—she was trouble.

Swilling back the water, he made himself relax his limbs.

It was ridiculous to get het up like this. She was leaving Yorkshire at the weekend, and that would be that. His mouth tightened. And Susan Richards had made it very plain she was up for a bit of fun with no strings attached. His perfect kind of woman, in fact.

His scowl deepened. When he replaced the empty glass on the table, it was with such force he was fortunate it didn't shatter.

CHAPTER THREE

WHATEVER had possessed her? Why had she challenged him like that? Gina stood, staring at her flushed reflection in the spotted little mirror in the ladies' cloakroom, mentally groaning. He had looked absolutely amazed, and no wonder.

Grabbing her bag, she hunted for her lip gloss and then stood with it in her hand, still staring vacantly. It had been his attitude that had done it. It had brought out the devil in her, and the temper that went with the hair. When she and her two sisters had been growing up, her father had repeatedly warned them about the folly of speaking first and thinking later—often lamenting the fact that he was the only male in a household of four red-haired women, while he'd been about it.

'A homebody.' And, 'you're bound to meet someone in London.' How patronising could you get? And why shouldn't she be a career woman, anyway? It wasn't only scrawny blondes like Susan Richards who had the monopoly on such things.

Suddenly she slumped, her eyes misty. She had behaved badly out there, and if she was being honest with herself it was because the sight of Harry and Susan had acted like salt on a raw wound.

Dabbing her eyes with a tissue, she sniffed loudly and then

repaired her make-up. This was all her own fault—she should never have come out to dinner with him. She had known it was foolish, worse than foolish, but she had done it anyway. Harry couldn't help being Harry. Being so drop-dead gorgeous, he was always going to have women panting after him, but at least after tonight she wouldn't have to watch it any longer.

The lurch her heart gave made her smudge the lip gloss down her chin. She stopped what she was doing and held herself round the middle, swaying back and forth a number of times, until the door opening brought her up straight.

A tall matronly looking woman entered, nodding and smiling at her before entering the one cubicle the tiny room held.

Gina wished she was old, or at least old enough for this to be past history. She wished she didn't love him so much. And more than anything she wished she wasn't so sure that she would never meet anyone who could stir her heart like Harry, which meant she wasn't likely to get the husband and children she'd always imagined herself having. She bit hard on her lip, her eyes cloudy. Harry was right. She *was* a homebody. And because of him she was being forced down a road she had never seen herself walking.

It was all his fault. She glared at her reflection, wiping her streaked chin, and then packing her make-up away. He was so content with his lot, so happy, so completely self-satisfied. The rat.

Taking a deep breath, she told herself to get a grip. He was buying her dinner, hardly a crime. And the watch was beautiful, made even more so by the fact he had noticed she wasn't wearing her old one. It had been kind of him to round off her time at Breedon & Son by taking her out, when all was said and done. So…no more griping. *Get yourself in there and be bright and sparkling, and leave him with a smile when the time comes.*

When Gina walked back into the dining area the sight of him caused her breath to catch in her throat, but then it always did. Which was at best annoying and worst embarrassing— like the time she had been eating a hot sausage-roll in the work canteen and had choked, until Natalie had slapped her on the back so hard she'd thought her spine had snapped in two.

She arrived at the table just as the waitress brought their main course, which was good timing. She could bury herself in the food to some extent, she thought, sliding into her seat and returning his smile. At least he *was* smiling now. He'd looked thoroughly irritated with her when she had left, and she couldn't altogether blame him.

'More wine?' He was refilling her glass as he spoke, and Gina didn't protest. She needed something to help her get through the evening without making a complete fool of herself, and in the absence of anything else alcohol would do. Although, that was flawed thinking, she told herself in the next moment. The wine was more likely to prompt her to do or say something silly.

Warning herself to go steady, she took a small sip and then tried the tagliatelle. It was delicious. The best she had ever tasted. Deciding that she was definitely a girl who would eat for comfort rather than pine away, she tucked in.

By the time the main course was finished, Gina had discovered that you could laugh and really mean it, even if your heart was on the verge of being broken. Harry seemed to put himself out to be the perfect dinner companion after their earlier blip, producing one amusing story after another, and displaying the wicked wit which had bowled her over in the first days of their acquaintance. Back then she had desperately been seeking a way to make him notice her as a woman; now that strain was taken off her shoulders at least. He saw her as a friend, and only as a friend, and she'd long since accepted it.

She chose pistachio meringue with fresh berries for dessert, and it didn't fail to live up to expectations. She didn't think she'd eat for a week after this evening, and she said so as she licked the last morsel of meringue off her spoon.

Harry grinned, his eyes following her pink tongue. 'I'm glad you enjoyed it. If I'd thought I could have introduced you to this place months ago.'

If he had thought. Quite. 'I'm glad you didn't. I'd be two stone heavier by now.'

'You could have taken your parents' dogs for a few extra walks and worked off the pounds,' he said easily.

'There speaks someone who's never had to diet.' Why would he? The man was perfect.

'Do you—have to diet, I mean?'

A bit personal, but she'd brought it on herself. Gina nodded. 'My sisters—wouldn't you just know?—follow after my dad, and he's a tall streak of nothing. My mother on the other hand is like me. We go on a diet every other week, but just as regularly fall by the wayside. My mum blames my dad for her lapses. She says he gives her no incentive because he likes her to be what he calls "cuddly".' She grimaced.

'I'm with your father.'

Gina smiled wryly.

'I mean it.'

Yeah, yeah, yeah. Purposely changing the subject, she said,

'Thank you for a lovely meal, Harry. I've really enjoyed it. It was a nice way to end my time at Breedon & Son.'

He seemed to digest that for a few seconds. 'It'll be odd, coming into work each day and you not being there.'

Be still, my foolish heart. She forced a smile. 'I think you'll find Susan a more than adequate replacement. She's very keen.' In more ways than one.

'I guess so.'

He didn't sound overly impressed, and Gina's heart jumped for joy before she reminded herself it meant nothing. If it wasn't Susan it would be someone else. Her voice even, she said, 'It'll all work out fine. Things always do, given time.' *Except me and you.*

'I think we're both long enough in the tooth to know that's not true,' he said drily. 'It goes hand in hand with accepting there's no Santa Clause.' He cleared his throat, his heavily lashed eyes intent on her face. 'Look, this is none of my business, and tell me to go to blazes if you want, but is this decision to leave Yorkshire anything to do with your personal life?'

She stared at him.

'You know what I mean,' he said after a moment. 'A man. Has a relationship ended unhappily, something like that? Because, if that's the reason, running away won't necessarily improve your state of mind.'

Panic stricken, she opened her mouth to deny it before logic stepped in. He had no idea the man in question was him, and if nothing else confirming his suspicions would work to her advantage. One, he'd have to accept she had a concrete reason for moving away, and two, it would explain her reluctance to visit in the future.

'I'm right, aren't I? Someone has let you down.'

After their earlier conversation, she couldn't bear the idea of Harry thinking she'd been discarded like an old sock. Stiffly, she said, 'It's not like that. *I* made the decision to end the relationship and move away.'

His eyes narrowed. She recognised the look on his face. It was one he adopted when he wouldn't take no for an answer on some business deal or other. It was this formidably tenacious streak in his nature that had seen Breedon & Son go from strength to strength in the last year since he'd come home. And that was great on a business level. Just dandy. It was vastly different when that acutely discerning mind was homed in on her, though. Recognising the wisdom of the old adage that pride went before a fall, she said quickly, 'It wasn't going anywhere, that's all. End of story.'

'What do you mean, not going anywhere? You're obviously upset enough about the finish of it to move away from your family and friends, your whole life,' he finished, somewhat dramatically for him. Then he added suddenly, 'He's not married, is he?'

'*Excuse me?*' It was a relief to hide behind outrage. 'I have never, and *would* never, get involved with someone else's husband.'

'No, of course you wouldn't.' He had the grace to look embarrassed. 'I know that, really I do. But what went wrong, then?'

Gina wondered if she could end this conversation with a few well-chosen words along the lines that he should mind his own business. But this was Harry she was dealing with. He was like one of those predatory fish of the Caribbean she'd read about recently: once it seized hold on something, it couldn't let go even if it wanted to. 'A common scenario,' she said as lightly as she could manage. 'He was content to jog along as we were indefinitely. I wanted more.'

He looked shocked. 'Did he know how much you cared for him?'

That was rich, coming from the man who—if office gossip was to be believed—discarded girlfriends like cherry stones once he'd enjoyed their fruit. Talk about a case of the pot calling the kettle black! Gina shrugged, keeping her voice steady and unemotional when she said, 'That's not really the point. We wanted different things for the future, that's all. I was ready to settle down, and he wasn't. Actually, I don't think he will ever settle down.'

He stared at her, a frown darkening his countenance. 'In other words, he strung you along?'

'No, he didn't string me along,' Gina said severely. 'He was always absolutely straight and above board, if you must know. I suppose I just...hoped for more.' And always had, from the first moment she had laid eyes on him. Always would, for that matter, if she didn't put a good few miles between them.

'You are being too kind. He must have known the sort of girl you are from the start.'

She couldn't do this any more. Her voice low, she said, 'Could we change the subject, please, Harry?'

He opened his mouth to object, but the waitress was at their side with the coffee. He waited until she had bustled off, and then spoke in a very patient tone, which had the effect of making her want to kick him. 'Believe me, Gina,' he said gently, 'I know the type of man he is, and he's not worthy of you.'

That was true at least. 'Really?' she said drily. 'You know this without even having met him?'

'Like I said, I know the type. Now, I'm not saying he's

wrong not to want to settle down, I'm the same way myself. But I wouldn't get involved with someone who had for ever on their mind, and there's the difference. And a man can tell. Always.'

He really was the most arrogant male on the planet. 'How?' 'How?'

'How can you tell if a woman is looking for something permanent or just a roll in the hay?' she asked baldly.

He looked askance at her. 'I hope it's never anything as crude as "just a roll in the hay",' he said stiffly. 'I'm a man, not an animal. I've never yet taken a woman just because she's indicated she's available.'

This self-righteous side of him was new. Gina fixed him with purposely innocent eyes. 'So you have to get to know someone first? Find out if they can provide mental as well as physical stimulation, perhaps? Make sure their slant on life and love is the same as yours?'

He stared at her as though he wasn't sure whether she was mocking him or not. After a moment, his eyes glinting, he said, 'You make it sound very cold-blooded.'

In for a penny, in for a pound. 'Perhaps because it is?' she suggested sweetly.

'I prefer to think of it as honest, and if this man you've been involved with had done the same you wouldn't be in the position you're in now,' he ground out somewhat grimly.

'But attraction, love, desire, doesn't always fit into nicely labelled little packages, does it?' Gina countered, the feeling that she'd hit him on the raw wonderfully satisfying. 'It can be a spontaneous thing, something that hits you wham-bang in the heart and takes you completely by surprise. Something so overpowering and real that everything and everyone else goes out of the window.'

He folded his arms over his chest, settling more comfortably in his seat as he studied her flushed face. 'It can be like that,' he agreed after some moments. 'But, if it is, things inevitably go wrong.'

'Of course they don't—'

'Was it like that for you with this man?' he interjected swiftly. 'A head-over-heels thing?'

She hesitated, and immediately he seized on it. 'You see?' he said coolly.

'What I *see* is that your attitude is a wonderful excuse for playing the field without fear of reprisals.'

'I beg your pardon?'

Refusing to be intimidated by his growl, Gina met his glare without flinching. 'You have the best of all worlds, Harry, you know you do. You can wine, dine and bed a woman as often as you like, and then walk away with a smile and a "I told you what to expect" when you've had enough. I find that…distasteful.'

'Distasteful?'

If the situation had been different, she could have laughed at the sheer outrage on his face. Funnily enough, his mounting temper had the effect of calming her. 'Yes, distasteful,' she said firmly. 'You can't tell me some of your girlfriends haven't fallen for you because, whatever modern thinking tries to promote, sex means more to a woman than a man in the emotional sense. Just the sheer mechanics of it means a woman allows—' She stopped abruptly as he raised a sardonic eyebrow.

'Yes?' he drawled with suspicious blankness.

'It means a woman allows a man into her body,' she said bravely, wondering why she was giving Harry—of all people—a biology lesson. 'Whereas, for a man…'

'It's possession, penetration?'

Ignoring her fiery cheeks, Gina nodded sharply. 'Exactly.'

'You don't think the man feels anything beyond physical satisfaction?'

'I didn't say that.' He knew she hadn't said that. 'But it *is* different.'

'*Vive la différence.*'

Her embarrassment seemed to have restored his equanimity. Drawing on her dignity, Gina said flatly, 'I'm sorry if you find it old-fashioned or amusing, but I happen to think that love should enter the equation however things turn out in the end. And I know there's no guarantee with any relationship; I'm not in cloud cuckoo land.'

He looked at her quietly for a moment. 'I wasn't laughing at you, Gina.'

And pigs fly.

'In fact the time was I might have expressed the same views myself, but—' He paused. 'People change. Life changes them.'

Gina said nothing. In truth she was startled by this last remark. His tone of voice, the look on his face, was different from anything that had gone before.

'I guess I've become self-sufficient, independent. I like my life the way it is, and to share it with another person would be at best inconvenient and worst a nightmare.'

She wished she'd never started this conversation. Breathing shallowly to combat the shaft of pain that had seared her chest, Gina said quietly, 'You missed out cynical.'

'You think I'm cynical?'

She nodded. 'Not just from what you've said tonight, but more over the last twelve months. I wonder, actually, if you really like women much, Harry.'

For a moment he didn't react at all. Then he said softly, 'I assure you, I'm not of the other persuasion.'

'No, I didn't mean—I—I know you're not—'

He cut short her stammerings with a dark smile, his voice self-mocking when he said, 'I know what you meant, Gina. It was my way of prevaricating.'

'Oh.' Sometimes his innate honesty was more than a little disturbing.

'Because you're right. I *am* cynical where the fair sex is concerned.'

Why was being proved right so horribly depressing? Hiding her feelings, Gina nodded slowly. Picking her words carefully, she said, 'Bad experience somewhere in your long-lost youth?' She hoped to defuse what had suddenly become an extremely charged atmosphere with her tone, knowing he wouldn't want to talk about it in any detail. The last year had proved he was a master at deflecting questions about his past.

This time he surprised her. Nodding, he leaned forward, taking one of the mints the waitress had brought with their coffee and unwrapping it before he said, 'Her name was Anna, and it was a wild, hot affair. We were crazy about each other at first, but we were young; I'd just left uni when we met. I thought it would go on for ever, made promises, you know? But after a year or so I found my feelings were beginning to change. I still loved her, cared about her, but I wasn't *in* love with her. That something had gone. Perhaps it had only ever been lust, I don't know.'

'And Anna?'

'She said she loved me with all her heart. Then she got sick. A rare form of cancer. Although, she wasn't. I only found out she'd lied to me after we'd married. One of her friends told me when she was drunk, she thought it was hilarious. I was a joke, apparently.'

'I'm sorry.' She was. His voice was painful to hear.

'So far from Anna only having a few short months to live, months she'd begged me to spend with her as man and wife, she was as healthy as the next person.'

'What did you do?'

'I told her I was leaving. That night she cut her wrists in the bath.'

Unable to believe her ears, Gina could only stare.

'And so it began. Months of manipulation and tears and threats and rages. Two more supposed suicide attempts when I was going to leave. Damn it, I was young, little more than a kid. I was in way over my head, and I was stupid. I really thought she might kill herself. Eventually it came to the point where I began to fear I was going mad. That was the point I walked out. Went abroad.'

'What…what did she do?'

He shrugged. 'Took me for every penny she could get, and made sure my name was mud, then married some other poor sop.'

Appalled, Gina reached out and touched his hand. 'She must have been sick.'

'Sick?' His lips twisted. 'No, I don't think Anna was sick. Manipulative, determined, cruel, hard—all under a cloak of fragile femininity, of course—but sick? I could have forgiven sick, but not the sheer resolve to get her own way no matter whom she trampled underfoot.'

And so he had decided never to get caught like that again. She could understand it. But surely he realised all women weren't like Anna? Quietly, she said, 'I think she was sick,

Harry. I've never met anyone like her. All the women I know would be horrified at what she did.'

He didn't argue the point. Draining his cup of coffee, he shrugged slowly as he replaced the cup on the saucer. 'You're probably right, but it doesn't matter anyway. Like I said, life changes people. She perhaps did me a favour, in the long run. I wouldn't have ended up in the States, maybe, wouldn't have decided what I wanted—and more importantly what I *didn't* want—so early on in life, but for Anna.'

'I'm sorry, but I don't think she did you a favour,' Gina said with more honesty than tact. 'How can living an autonomous life be a favour? You'll miss out on a wife, children—'

'I don't want a wife and children, Gina,' he said calmly and coolly. 'I have what I want, and I consider myself most fortunate.'

She could have believed him one hundred per cent, but for the shadow darkening the smoky-grey eyes. And then he blinked and it was gone. Perhaps she'd imagined it in the first place. Gathering all her courage, she said, 'And what you want is a beautiful empty shell of a house, with no family to make it a home? Not ever? A life of complete independence with no one to grow old with, no one to look back over the years with? No one to cuddle when the night's dark and morning's a long way off?'

For several seconds, seconds that shivered with a curious intimacy, he held her gaze. Then the grey eyes closed against her. When he looked up again, he was smiling, his voice holding an amused note when he said, 'You're a romantic, Gina Leighton.'

How the knowledge that he wasn't smiling inside had come, Gina wasn't sure, but it was there. She didn't smile back, her face sweetly solemn as her eyes searched the sharply defined planes and angles of the hard male features.

'I believe in love,' she said softly. 'I believe in the sort of love between a man and a woman that has the potential to go on for a lifetime, and nothing else can measure up to the contentment and wonder of it. It has the power to sweep away barriers of culture and religion, heal unhealable hurts, and mend broken hearts. It can change the most dyed-in-the-wool cynic for the better and make the world a place worth living in. Yes, I believe all that, and if that fits your definition of a romantic then I hope up my hands and plead guilty, gladly.'

Harry shook his head slowly. 'And all this when the man you wanted to spend the rest of your life with has let you walk away?'

She blinked. That had been below the belt, and it hurt. Lots.

'I'm sorry.' Immediately he reached out and took her hand, holding on to her fingers when she would have pulled away. A thousand nerves responded to the feel of his warm flesh, and as she closed her eyes against the flood of desire his voice came, low and repentant. 'I'm really sorry, Gina. That was unforgivable. I'm the sort of primeval animal that attacks when it's threatened.'

Threatened? Bewildered, she met his gaze. For once his face was open, even vulnerable, and it betrayed something: a need, a longing. For what, she didn't know, but it was there in the smoky depths of the grey eyes. She swallowed hard. 'You objected to my placing you on a par with an animal earlier,' she reminded him, managing a fair attempt at a smile.

'So I did.'

She could read the relief in his face. He hated emotional scenes. She knew the reason for that now. 'Can I have my hand back, please?' she said with the sort of cheerfulness he expected of her. 'I want to drink my coffee.'

'Sure.' He grinned at her, and her heart writhed. She couldn't imagine not seeing him every day. She hadn't tried to, knowing it would weaken her resolve if she did. But now the time was here. In a little while, maybe an hour or two, he would happily drive out of her life without a care in the world. He'd perhaps even sing along to the car radio or one of his CD's on the way home, feeling he'd done his duty to the stalwart secretary who had babysat him in his first weeks at work.

She wondered what he'd do if she succumbed to the sudden temptation to tell him how she felt. To ask him to kiss her, really kiss her, just once. For old times' sake, or whatever he wanted to call it.

He'd be horrified. The answer was there with bells on. Horrified, embarrassed, alarmed. And every time he thought of her from now on—if he ever did, of course—it would be with awkwardness and discomfiture. And she didn't want that. OK, it was probably her pride again, but she would really rather walk through coals of fire than have him mentally squirm if her name came to mind.

'…your address?'

'I'm sorry?' Too late she realised he'd been talking, and she hadn't heard a word.

He shook his head. 'You were thinking of him just now, weren't you?' he accused. 'This guy who's let you down. Are you seeing him again before you leave for London?'

He seemed put out, but she couldn't think why. It was no skin off Harry's nose whether she saw her imaginary lover or not. She shrugged. 'I'm not sure,' she said dismissively. She'd discussed this whole thing enough, besides which she was worried she might trip herself up. Lying didn't come naturally to her, and she knew she was extremely bad at it. 'And he didn't let me down, not like you mean. What did you say before?' she added, before he started to argue the point.

'I said, you'll have to remember to give me your address and telephone number tonight,' he said.

A trifle sullenly, Gina thought. But then Harry never had been able to stand being disagreed with. She nodded. She had no intention of giving Harry her address in London after his comment earlier in the day about dossing down on her sofa if he was in town. She'd make some excuse when he dropped her off, saying she'd post it to him, something like that. And she wasn't going to delay their goodbye, either. She didn't want his last sight of her to be one of her howling her head off.

They finished their coffee and mints, and Harry paid the bill. Gina's heart was beating a tattoo as they walked out to the car, Harry's hand at her elbow. The night was scented with spring and to Gina's heightened emotions, unbearably lovely. She didn't think she had ever felt so miserable in the whole of her life.

Once in the car, Harry didn't start the engine immediately. Instead he twisted in his seat to look at her, frowning slightly. 'I'm worried about you, Gina,' he said quietly.

She became aware her mouth had fallen open, and shut it quickly. If he'd suddenly taken all his clothes off and danced in the moonlight, she couldn't have been more surprised. More thrilled, certainly, but not more surprised. 'I don't follow,' she hedged warily.

'This taking off to London to nurse a broken heart. It's dangerous. You're leaving yourself wide open for the worse sort of guy to take advantage of you. Away from friends and family, all alone in the bit city, you'll be incredibly vulnerable.'

He made her sound like Little Orphan Annie. She stared at him for a moment before she said stiffly, 'I'm thirty-two years old, Harry. Not sweet sixteen.'

'What's that got to do with it?'

'Everything.'

His mouth set in the stubborn pout he did so well. It made her toes curl, but she wasn't about to betray that to this big, hard, sexy man. Just occasionally—like now—she caught a glimpse of what the boy Harry must have looked like, and it was intoxicating. But Harry was no callow youth. He was an experienced and ruthlessly intelligent man who would capitalise on any weakness an opponent revealed. She'd seen him too often in action on the business front to be fooled.

'I don't think you've thought this through,' he said flatly, after a few tense moments had ticked by.

'Excuse me?' She couldn't believe the cheek of it. She hadn't thought it through? She'd done nothing else for months. Months when he'd been busy getting up close and personal with some blonde or other. He clearly didn't only see her as unattractive and sexless, but stupid as well. 'What on earth would you know about it?' she said stonily.

'Don't get on your high horse.' He seemed unaffected by her obvious rage. 'I'm merely pointing out you're on the rebound, because anyone who *is* on the rebound never makes allowance for it.'

Agony aunt as well—there was no limit to his attributes. Gina glared at the man she loved with every fibre of her being. 'So, you've pointed it out,' she said frostily. 'Feel better?'

'If you've taken it on board?'

'Oh, of course I have,' she said sarcastically. '*You* said it, after all.'

'Very funny.' He started the car engine. 'I'm only trying to look out for a friend. What's wrong with that?'

A grey bleakness settled on her. 'Nothing,' she said flatly. 'Thanks.'

'My pleasure.' He swung the car out of the tiny car park and on to the road, the darkness settling round them as only country darkness can.

Gina sat absolutely still, staring out of the windscreen, but without seeing the road in front of them. She felt shattered, emotionally, mentally and physically. The countless sleepless nights she'd endured over the last months as she'd agonised about Harry, the build up to today which she'd been dreading, the surprise invitation to have dinner with him—and not least their conversation throughout—had all served to bring her to a state of exhaustion. And of course all the wine she'd drunk had added to the overall stupor she was feeling, she thought drily, shutting her eyes and relaxing back against the seat.

She didn't know if she had actually dropped off or not when she became aware Harry had brought the car to a halt. She opened her eyes to find they were still deep in country and darkness. 'What is it?' she asked in some alarm as he began to reverse along the narrow lane they'd been travelling down.

'I'm not sure.' He glanced at her. 'Go back to sleep. This isn't a "I've run out of petrol" scenario.'

No, more's the pity. 'I never thought it was,' she said, her voice holding the ring of truth.

He reversed some hundred yards or so before pulling up. 'I saw a car start off from this point, and as we passed I saw a cardboard box by the side of the verge. I just want to look in it.'

'Look in it?'

He nodded, his voice somewhat sheepish as he said, 'I don't know why, but I've got a funny feeling about it. Stay in the car.' He opened the driver's door and climbed out, Gina following a second later. He was already bending over the box, and before he opened it he said, 'I said stay in the car.'

'Don't be silly.' She came round the bonnet. 'What's in it?'

'Hell.' He'd lifted the lid as she had been speaking, and now as she reached him and looked down she saw several tiny shapes moving and squeaking.

'Oh, Harry.' She clutched his sleeve, her eyes wide and horrified. 'Someone's dumped some puppies. Out here, in the middle of nowhere. How could they?'

'Quite easily, it seems,' he said grimly.

'Are they all right?' They were both crouching down by the box now, and could make out four puppies in the moonlight, wriggling about on folded newspaper and smeared with their own excrement. 'Oh, poor little things.' Gina was nearly crying. 'What are we going to do?'

Harry stood up. 'If I put the car blanket over your knee, could you have the box on your lap?'

'Of course. Anything, anything.' She couldn't believe someone had actually been so heartless as to put the puppies in a box, bring them to a deserted spot and just drive off. Not with all the sanctuaries that took unwanted litters these days.

Once they were back in the car again, the box on her lap, Gina peered in. 'They're very small,' she said shakily. 'Do you think there's something the matter with them?'

'Not with the racket they're making,' Harry said drily.

'Where are we going to take them?'

'There must be a vet somewhere around here, but I haven't

got a clue where. Look, my cleaner, Mrs Rothman, has dogs. Do you mind if we retrace our footsteps so to speak, and call on her? If nothing else she might be able to point us in the right direction. It'll mean you're late back, though. We're halfway back to your place.'

She hadn't realised they'd travelled so far. He was right. She *had* been asleep. 'It doesn't matter about being late. I haven't got to get up for work in the morning, remember? It'll be a cleaning and sorting day, so please do go and see your Mrs Rothman.' At least she'd have extra time with him. Not that she would have wished it at the cost of someone dumping the puppies, but still…

The puppies quietened down as the warmth of the car kicked in, but this had the effect of causing Gina to check them every couple of minutes, terrified they'd died. It was a huge relief when eventually they came to the small village, which was a stone's throw from Harry's secluded cottage, and drew up outside a neat terraced house.

Mrs Rothman proved to be a plump, motherly type who drew them into the warmth of her smart little house and insisted on her husband making them all a cup of tea while she oohed and ahhed over the contents of the box. 'Jack Russell crosses, by the look of it,' she announced once she'd inspected the puppies. 'All females. I bet whoever owned the bitch could get rid of the males but not the females. Happens like that sometimes. Or maybe it was just a huge litter.'

After cleaning the four little scraps up, Mrs Rothman lined the box with fresh newspaper while her husband mushed up some of their dog food. The puppies made short if somewhat messy work of it, after which Mrs Rothman popped them back in the box on top of an old towel. All four promptly went to sleep, clearly worn out by their unwelcome adventure.

'How old do you think they are?' Gina asked Mrs Rothman once she and Harry and the older couple were sitting sipping a second cup of tea in front of the blazing coal-fire, the puppies snuggled together in their box to one side of the hearth.

'Hard to tell, but they managed the food fairly well, so I'd say about six weeks or so, maybe seven or eight. They wouldn't have lasted long, left where they were. The nights can still be bitter.' Mrs Rothman turned to Harry. 'I know of a dog sanctuary not far from here. I'll give you the telephone number and address. They'll take them, I'm sure.'

Harry nodded. 'Thanks.'

One of the puppies began to squeak with little piping sounds, and Gina knelt down and lifted the squirming little body out of the box and onto her lap, stroking the silky fur until it went back to sleep again. Harry looked at her. 'I know,' he said. 'What sort of so-and-so could watch them grow to this stage and then leave them to die?'

It was exactly what she had been thinking, and his understanding brought tears to her eyes. That and the fact that she could see he too was deeply affected by the puppies' plight. As another one began to scrabble about, he fetched it out of the box and fussed over it until it settled on his lap.

Mrs Rothman plied them with more tea and a slice of her home-made seed cake, the fire crackled and glowed, the puppies slept, and the big grandfather clock in a corner of the room ticked on. It was cosy and warm, and Gina didn't want the moment ever to end.

And then Harry stood up. 'Right,' he said briskly, depositing his puppy back with her sisters. 'We've bothered you long enough. If you could let me have the address of the sanctuary, and a tin of dog food to tide them over until I drop them off, we'll be on our way.'

The brief interlude was over.

CHAPTER FOUR

HARRY was experiencing a whole host of emotions new to him, and none of them was welcome.

This evening had been a mistake of gigantic proportions from start to finish, he thought grimly as he and Gina made their goodbyes and walked to the car, the box tucked under his arm, and Gina carrying a bag containing several tins of dog food which Mrs Rothman insisted on pressing on them. And finding the puppies had been the icing on the whole damn cake.

Once he'd settled Gina in the car with the box on her lap, he walked round the bonnet to the driver's side.

Gina Leighton was beautiful, sweet, intelligent and heart-wrenchingly vulnerable, and a woman like that definitely didn't feature in his life. No way. With someone like Gina came commitment, responsibilities, ties, problems, and he was done with such things for good. He'd rather jump out of a plane without a parachute than ever consider travelling down that road again in a hundred lifetimes.

Once in the car, the puppies were yelping and mewing and scrabbling about in the box like crazy. 'I think they want their mum,' Gina said as he pulled on his seat belt. 'They must wonder what on earth is happening.'

He knew how they felt. Life had seemed so straightforward this morning. He'd thought that if she followed through on actually leaving—which he'd doubted till the last moment—than a warm goodbye, a little word about the watch and all she'd done for him and how grateful he was, and that would be that. Pleasant departure. Smiles all round. Simple. Clean.

So why had he asked her to have dinner with him? He went to start the car, but one of the puppies made a good attempt at using her sisters as a springboard to catapult on to the rim of the box, causing Gina to squeal before she said quickly, 'Sorry. She made me jump.'

'Nimble little blighters, aren't they?' Harry couldn't help smiling. Abandoned they might be. Quitters they most certainly were not.

'How are you going to travel all the way back from my place without them escaping in the car?' Gina tilted her head at him. 'Wouldn't it be simpler to take them to your house first and settle them somewhere, in the kitchen maybe, before you take me home? Or I could call a taxi. Or, failing that, I'll have them and take them to the sanctuary in the morning.'

He stared at her. None of the women he'd seen over the last few years would have been bothered about him in this situation—or the puppies come to that. Their prime concern would have been their clothes, hair, nails—in that order.

Then he shook himself mentally. He was probably being grossly unfair to the odd one or two. But only the odd one or two. 'It might be a good idea to nip home and put them in the utility room before I take you back,' he admitted. 'The boiler's in there, so it's always warm, and I've got some bits of wood in the garage I can use to pen them in and contain them. It'll give them room to be comfortable.'

She nodded. 'Do that, then.' She gave a weak giggle. 'But quickly. This big one is determined to make a break for it. She's obviously got leadership qualities.'

He smiled back at her. 'There's always one…'

As he started the car, Gina said, 'They're very sweet, aren't they? And that puppy smell. It's gorgeous.'

'It wasn't so gorgeous before Mrs Rothman cleaned them up,' Harry said practically.

She giggled again. He wondered why such a simple, innocent sound should make him so sexually excited. But then, if he was truthful, he'd been fighting the attraction this woman held for him since day one. Her soft, generous curves, the pale, ginger-speckled skin, that mass of silky hair that shone with myriad shades of red and copper when a shaft of sunshine touched it…

He swung the car on to the road, driving automatically, taken up with his thoughts. Sometimes he'd only had to walk into the office and see Gina sitting demurely at her desk to become as hard as a rock. If she knew the sexual fantasies he'd indulged in… The situation had annoyed him, irritated him on occasion, and certainly disturbed him not a little. It had also frightened the dickens out of him, he realised with a little shock of self-awareness.

If she'd been some brassy, hard-boiled piece it would all have been different. They could have enjoyed each other's bodies for as long as it had taken for the attraction to burn itself out. If she *was* attracted to him, that was. He frowned to himself. He'd thought there was a spark between them, but he might be fooling himself here. She'd always been the model of decorum. Damn it, it was an impossible situation. Which was why he had to admit to an initial feeling of relief when she'd said she was leaving.

Did he still feel relief? The car headlights caught a fox crossing the road in front of them, the animal's red fur and thick bushy tail disappearing into the shadows in the next instant.

He wasn't sure what he felt any more. He wanted to take her to bed, no question of that. He did not want a woman in his life permanently, set in concrete. And now she had revealed she was leaving because of a man which, he was forced to acknowledge, had thrown him somewhat. It had been a long time since he'd felt the nasty little gremlin of jealousy jabbing at him, but it had been there tonight. Their whole conversation had made him realise he didn't know Gina as well as he'd thought he did.

She'd said the man wasn't married, and he believed her. Gina wouldn't lie. But selfish he most certainly was. She had clearly been seeing him for a long time, and to let her walk away the way he had… A muscle contracted in his jaw. He'd love five minutes alone with the swine.

Another little squeal from Gina brought his eyes to her as she carefully pushed the biggest puppy down in the box again. 'We're nearly home,' he said, just as he swung the car off the road and on to his drive.

'Not before time.' She glanced at him as he drew up outside the cottage. 'How are you going to get them to the sanctuary in the morning? This box won't be any good.'

'I'll find something else. Failing that, a generous contribution to the place might persuade someone to come out and fetch them.'

Once in the cottage, he left Gina in the utility room with the puppies while he went to the garage and sorted out a couple of pieces of wood. When he returned, it was to find her kneeling on the tiles with the puppies scampering about her.

'They're so cute.' She glanced up at him, her eyes alight, and his stomach muscles registered her tousled softness. 'I thought they were all the same at first, but one's bigger than the others, and that one—' she pointed '—is smaller, and the other two are the same size.'

He nodded. 'There are two puddles on the floor,' he said.

She grimaced. 'They can't help that, they're only babies. Aren't you?' she added, lifting the smallest puppy into her arms and stroking the small, downy head. 'You're just little babies without your mum. Take no notice of moany old Harry.'

Harry fought down the urge to take her straight upstairs into his bed, and show her that there was pleasure and enjoyment and life after this rat who had let her down. Instead he positioned the wood so it effectively enclosed a third of the utility room, spreading a wad of newspapers in one corner in the hope further puddles would be kept to one spot. In another corner, he made a bed of towels.

In the meantime Gina had wandered into the kitchen and found a couple of saucers, one of which she filled with water and one with pulped dog-food. The minute she came back and put them down, the puppies were on them.

They stood for a good few minutes, watching them feed and explore their new surroundings, laughing at their antics.

They really were four little clowns, Harry thought as he watched the smallest puppy hanging onto the biggest one's tail by its teeth, before she was bowled over by one of the others. He'd grown up with dogs, but his parents had always chosen ones on the large side—Labradors and German Shepherds. These little mites were quite different, but seemed full of personality.

A stifled yawn at the side of him brought him back to the

realisation it was very late. He glanced at his watch and was amazed to see it was after one o'clock. 'Why don't you stay the night?' he said suddenly.

'What?'

Gina looked as startled as he felt, he told himself with dark humour. Where on earth had that invitation come from?

'Stay the night,' he repeated quietly. 'It's very late, and you're obviously dead beat. It seems sensible to stay here.'

He saw her mouth open and close. Something in the blue eyes made him sure she was going to refuse, and he added quickly, 'Mrs Rothman always keeps the guest-room bed aired and made up.'

He saw her swallow. 'I couldn't.'

'Why?'

'Why?' She appeared lost for words for a moment. 'Because I've loads to do in the morning.'

That wasn't the true story. His mouth dried. He'd bet his bottom dollar she'd arranged to see Lover Boy in the morning. Perhaps before this guy went into work. Damn it, couldn't she see this man was just using her? Perhaps he even expected a *bon-voyage* quickie. Without a shred of remorse for the crudity, he said carefully, 'You'll be home first thing—I've got to go to work, don't forget. Perhaps we could even drop the puppies off at this sanctuary on the way. That'd be a great help to me. In fact, I don't know how I'm going to manage it without you.'

She stared at him, her blue eyes dark with some emotion he couldn't fathom. She was probably weighing up the pain and pleasure of seeing Lover Boy compared to lending him a hand. Feeling he needed to press his cause, he said gently, 'Like you said, they're just little babies without their mum.

I'd hate for things to be more difficult than they need to be in the morning, and handling the four of them might prove a problem.' Deciding the end justified the means, he lied through his teeth as he added, 'You're used to dogs. I'm not.'

He saw her eyes narrow and realised he'd overdone it when she said, 'I thought you once told me your parents have always had dogs?'

They had had too many long chats over coffee breaks. Recovering quickly, he smiled. 'That's true, but I left home well over a decade ago, besides which these little things bear no resemblance to the sort of dogs I grew up with.'

'Mrs Rothman thought they were Jack Russell crossed with fox terriers, something like that. They're not exactly going to be tiny dogs.'

'But they're tiny now. And wriggly.' He wondered how far he could push the helpless-male scenario.

Gina glanced from him to the puppies, who were now quiet again, curled up together and looking pathetically helpless on their bed of towelling. Knowing her soft heart, he murmured, 'I'd hate to drop one of them.'

He saw her shut her eyes for an infinitesimal second. Whether it was with despair at his feebleness, or irritation at her predicament, he wasn't sure.

'All right,' she said ungraciously. 'I'll stay. But I need to be away first thing.'

Definitely expecting a visit from the rat. 'Sure thing. I don't want to be late. Busy day in front of me tomorrow, and Susan's not clued up on things like you are, although she's doing great.'

'Isn't she?' Gina said.

He could tell she was still mad at being trapped here,

because there was an edge to her voice. 'Want a cup of coffee or anything before we turn in?'

'Do you have any cocoa?'

'Cocoa?' he asked in surprise.

She flushed. 'I usually have a mug of milky cocoa in bed,' she said a trifle defensively.

Dampening down a mental image of Gina sitting up in bed stark-naked, her hair about her shoulders while her pink tongue licked at the froth on top of a mug of cocoa, Harry cleared his throat. His voice husky, he said, 'Sorry, no cocoa, but there's plenty of milk. How about a mug of hot milk instead—will that do?'

Gina nodded. He thought she looked very unhappy, and a mixture of anger and resentment slashed through him. Anger at this no-good character she was mixed up with. Resentment that someone he had thought so sensible and discriminating could allow themselves to be treated this way. The sooner she was well away from Yorkshire, the better. And yet he didn't want her to go. How much he didn't want her to go he hadn't realised until just this very moment.

Feeling confused, he led the way into the kitchen. Gina perched on a stool and watched him as he placed two mugs on the breakfast bar, and then poured a pint of milk into a saucepan. 'I'll join you in the milk,' he said obsequiously, aiming to get into her good books.

She nodded but didn't comment.

'And I appreciate you staying and helping with the puppies in the morning.'

His tone had been light, and he saw her rouse herself and stitch a smile on her face. 'I couldn't leave a mere male to cope with four offspring, now, could I?'

'True.' He'd never noticed just how superb her legs were before, but with her sitting on that stool he was probably seeing more of them than usual. Ignoring the stirring in his body, he said cheerfully, 'At least babies of the animal variety don't necessitate the use of nappies.'

'Nappies are no problem these days, even to the most incompetent man. There's no pins or folding them over in a certain way. It's all done for you. You just stick two tabs together, and job's a good 'un.'

'I'll take your word for it,' he said drily.

'Don't tell me—you believe nappy changing and the rest of it is women's work.'

'Actually, I don't,' he said mildly.

'No?' Her lifted eyebrows expressed her disbelief.

'No. If a couple decide to take on the enormous responsibility of bringing a new life into the world, then it's a joint decision all the way, or should be. Taking it as read that certain functions can only be performed by a mother—breast-feeding, for example…I think parenthood should be a fifty-fifty undertaking.' He poured the milk into the mugs.

'Oh.'

'You don't believe me?' he asked, turning to look at her.

'I didn't say that,' she protested quietly.

'You didn't have to. You had a funny look on your face.'

Her face cleared of all expression. 'I can't help my face,' she said with a weak smile. 'So you're a new-age man, then?'

'Ah, now that's a different question. I only said having a child should be a mutual undertaking, not that I'd consider it for myself.'

She nodded. 'No, of course not. You're strictly autonomous. You take what you want when you want, and then move on.'

He'd been in the process of handing a mug of milk to her, and for a moment his body stilled before carrying on. 'Is that how you see me?' he asked very quietly, a surge of emotion warning him he needed to control his temper.

She stared at him, her eyes unreadable. 'That's the picture you've presented to me.'

'I don't think so.'

Shrugging, she said, 'Perhaps you should listen to yourself some time, Harry.'

'I don't need to, damn it. I know what I am and how I think.' Or he had, up till this evening. Glaring at her, he growled, 'I'm not some sort of conscienceless stud, Gina.'

'That's fine, then,' she said flatly, her expression inscrutable.

He didn't know if he wanted to shake her or kiss her, he thought rawly, fighting down an anger he would never have acknowledged had its roots in hurt. 'We've known each other for twelve months, and for most of that time we've met every working day. We've talked and laughed and shared about our lives, and you can honestly say you see me like that?' he asked intensely.

She hesitated, putting down her mug and letting her eyelashes sweep down over her eyes for some moments, before she looked at him again. Her voice soft, she said, 'I don't want to make you angry, Harry, but I think most of the sharing—at least regarding past history—came from me. And that's fine, I wouldn't want to force a confidence from anyone, but you didn't really give anything of yourself. And before you fire off at me, think about it.'

He sat back on his stool, genuinely amazed.

'You're a very private man, and after what you told me about Anna and everything I can understand why you don't want to be involved with anyone. But…' She cleared her throat. 'Sex doesn't equate to much the way you view it. Fact.'

He stated the obvious. 'The women I take to bed know the score.'

'Yes, I know. You've already explained that.'

Silence hung between them like a pulsing entity. He was aware his body was taut with the effort to appear relaxed and unconcerned, and suddenly he threw pretense to one side and said simply, 'I don't like the way you see me, Gina.'

Something in her face changed, and her voice was throaty when she murmured, 'I'm sorry, I shouldn't have said all that. Your life is your own, and I've got no right to criticise one way or the other.'

Was she thinking of this man and the mess she'd made of her own life? So swiftly that it surprised him, his anger was gone, replaced with a desire to comfort her. 'You're probably closer to me than anyone else on earth,' he said quietly. 'So of course you have the right to state your opinion.'

He saw her face contract as though with pain, and felt a growing fury towards the unknown man who had broken her heart, and a surge of protectiveness. 'You're too good for him, you know that, don't you?'

'What?'

Her eyes widened in confusion, and he saw she hadn't followed him. Slightly embarrassed, he said gently, 'You'll meet someone, Gina, and all this will be like a bad dream.'

Her pent-up breath escaped in a little sigh. Shaking her head, she whispered, 'I'm not banking on it. You didn't meet someone else. And anyway, we were talking about you, not me.' She drained the last of her milk and slid off the stool, wisps of hair about her cheeks, and smudges of tiredness staining the pale skin beneath the dark pools of her eyes. 'Could you show me my room?'

A shiver of desire flickered through his blood. He wanted her. More badly than he had wanted any woman. Possibly because he had waited longer for her than anyone else. But, no, it wasn't just that. If it had been just that it would have been easily dealt with. But this was Gina. He not only wanted her but he—His mind came to an abrupt stop, a door slamming shut. He liked her, he finished silently. As a friend. And you didn't take friends to bed.

He stood up, managing a creditable smile. 'Sure.'

When they reached the stairs Harry stood aside for her to precede him, his eyes on her very nicely rounded bottom as he followed her to the landing. By the time they reached her room, he was deep in the grip of an erotic fantasy that was causing problems with a certain part of his anatomy.

'It's lovely.' Gina glanced round the room after he had opened the door and waved her through. She turned, smiling politely. 'Goodnight, then.'

Struggling with his self-induced state of arousal, Harry said thickly, 'Goodnight, Gina. You'll find towels and toiletries and so on in the *en suite;* Mrs Rothman likes to keep everything ready just in case. I'll give you a knock twenty minutes or so before breakfast, OK?'

'Thank you.' She hesitated, and then said in a rush, 'And thank you for offering me a bed for the night. I didn't sound very grateful down there, did I?'

'Why should you? It's you doing me the favour, not the other way round.' Actually he was doing her a massive favour in keeping her from the love rat, but she'd never see it even if he came clean. He watched her rub her small, cute nose, something she did when she was uncertain or wary. He realised there were lots of little things he knew about her.

'Well, thanks anyway,' she repeated.

She was clearly waiting for him to go, so why did he feel glued to the spot? Softly, he said, 'Sleep well, Gina.' And, even knowing it was a mistake, he bent forward and brushed her lips with his.

As kisses went it was fleeting, but the scent of her, the softness of her half-parted lips, produced a reaction that rocked him to his core. Desire, primitive and raw, shot through him and it took all of his control to turn away and walk towards the stairs. He heard the door close as he reached them, and stopped, closing his eyes and resting one hand on the banister as he drew in a hard, shaky breath.

Crazy. Everything about tonight was crazy. Crazy conversations. Crazy feelings. *Crazy situation.*

It would be different in the morning, in the cold, bright light of day. He opened his eyes, his face hardening. It would have to be.

CHAPTER FIVE

GINA didn't know when she became aware that the sound in her dream was actually real. She lay in a state of muzzy half-awareness for a while, unable to come round fully, and then sat up in bed as reality hit. She was in Harry's home, in his bed. Well, not in *his* bed, but in one of his beds.

Switching on the bedside lamp, she reached for her watch which she'd placed on the little cabinet earlier. Half-past three. And she knew she'd still been awake at three o'clock. She'd probably only had twenty minutes of sleep; no wonder she felt so out of it.

It was the puppies. The sound that had woken her was still there, a distant whining and yelping, and now she tiredly brushed the hair out of her eyes and reached for the towelling robe she'd found on the back of the *en suite* door. She'd have to go and see what was the matter. Harry was probably a typical man; once he was asleep nothing short of an earthquake would stir him. Her father could sleep through anything.

She sat on the edge of the bed for a few moments once she'd pulled the robe on, feeling distinctly light-headed. Probably due to the storm of weeping that had ensued once she'd been by herself earlier, she thought dismally. And crying while trying not to make a sound had given her a headache. She'd hunt about for some aspirin while she was downstairs, but first she'd better see what was what in the utility room.

Considering she'd been a stranger to them a few short hours ago, the puppies gave her a rapturous welcome when she padded into the utility room, tumbling over each other in an effort to reach her. Laughing despite her tiredness, she changed the top layer of newspaper, where they'd obligingly done their duties, and then prepared some more food which they polished off in record time.

'You were hungry.' She looked down at them as they moved round the now-empty saucer, small pink tongues still licking for traces of food.

The smallest puppy made her way over to her, beginning to nibble at her toes as the others scrabbled round for attention. 'You want some fuss, is that it?' Curling up on the wad of towelling Harry had put down, Gina allowed the four little warm bodies to make their way on to her lap. 'Missing Mum and home, I suppose,' she murmured as she stroked their furry heads. 'Although, if you did but know it, you're far better off here. Who knows what would have happened to you if Harry hadn't noticed that box?'

'It's ten to four.'

Harry's voice from the doorway brought her head jerking up so fast, she heard her neck crack. He was standing leaning against the wall; she didn't know how long he'd been watching her.

'I know.' Her mouth had gone dry. He was dressed in dark pyjama-bottoms and a black-cotton robe which was hanging loose. His thickly muscled chest was black with body hair, and

his hair was tousled and falling over his brow. He looked...
magnificent. 'It was the puppies,' she mumbled feverishly.
'They were crying. They were hungry.'

'You should have ignored them.'

'I couldn't.' The virile masculinity just feet away reminded
her she was stark naked under her robe. She wanted to tighten
the belt, but with her arms full of puppies she couldn't.
'Anyway, you came down too, I wasn't the only one.'

'True.'

He didn't elaborate as to whether she had disturbed him or
he'd been awake anyway. She was aware he was looking at
her with unconcealed scrutiny, and she wished she'd taken the
time to at least brush her hair. She'd scrubbed at her face
before she had gone to sleep in an effort to remove the last of
the make-up her tears hadn't washed away; she bet her nose
was shining like Rudolph's. When the smallest puppy made
a valiant attempt to bury herself inside the top of her robe,
thereby causing it to gape a little, Gina hastily tipped the four
of them off her lap and pulled the belt tight.

Carefully rising to her feet, she said nervously, 'I'm sorry
if I woke you.'

'You didn't.'

She expected him to move from the doorway as she approached, and when he didn't she stopped a foot or so away,
praying the trembling deep inside wasn't visible.

'You've washed your face,' he said slowly.

'Yes.' She didn't need to be reminded of what she must
look like.

'I can see your freckles better,' he observed, as though that
had been the whole point of the exercise.

She wrinkled her nose. 'Don't remind me.'

'I like freckles, especially with blue eyes and reddish-gold hair.'

'Titian,' she corrected automatically, glad he hadn't said 'ginger'.

'Titian,' he repeated softly. 'But your eyelashes are dark brown. And thick.'

She'd always been glad about that. It was one of the few things about herself she liked. She tried to think of something to say, something witty and light, and failed utterly. It was the look on his face. He was staring at her as though she was a woman. Which she was, of course. It was just that he had never noticed before.

But this was Harry. The warning screamed through her head. Harry, the self-determining. Harry, the mother and father of non-involvement. Harry, who didn't want a woman in his life other than to take care of his sexual needs. And that was what was happening right now, or would happen if she let it. She loved him too much to become just another notch on his bedpost. She wouldn't be able to stand it when he dropped her off later in the morning with a cheery wave and a casual goodbye. Because that's what he'd do.

Lowering her head, she tightened the belt of her robe still more. 'Fancy a cup of tea?' she said, hearing herself with a touch of hysteria. Tea. *Tea?*

There was a brief pause, and then his voice came cool and easy. 'If there's toast to go with it. I'm starving.'

So was she, but not for tea and toast. But she'd had her chance and blown it, she thought with burning regret.

The puppies had settled down again, all but the smallest, who now had her two front paws scrabbling at the wood barrier as she whimpered pitifully. Glad of the diversion, Gina retraced her footsteps and lifted the little scrap into her arms, whereupon the puppy immediately snuggled against her and shut its eyes.

'What?' she challenged as she caught Harry's eyes. 'The poor little thing's due some cuddles after all she's been through.' She was also a welcome third-party if they were going to indulge in tea and toast.

'Will you spoil your children, too?' he murmured smokily, amusement colouring his voice.

'With cuddles, if they're frightened or upset?' she said tartly, ignoring the pang her heart gave. She would never have children because they couldn't be Harry's. 'Absolutely.'

Once in the kitchen with the puppy cradled against her chest, she didn't try to clamber onto a stool, but stood and watched him as he filled the kettle and then placed two slices of bread in the toaster. 'Mind if I go through to the sitting room?' she asked as casually as she could. 'My feet are cold on these tiles.'

'Be my guest. I'll bring the tray through in a minute or two.'

There was a dark stubble on his chin. He was as unlike the perfectly groomed, smooth operator of daylight hours as the man in the moon. And a hundred times more dangerous.

Tingling with something she didn't want to put a name to, Gina made her way to the sitting room and chose a big, plumpy chair to curl up in, carefully positioning her feet under her and making sure the robe was discreetly in place. The puppy stirred briefly and then settled itself again as Gina gently stroked the plump little body. She gazed down at the sleeping animal, a sense of surrealism taking hold.

How on earth had she come to be in this position? Practically naked—apart from one piece of cloth—in Harry's house at four o'clock in the morning, with him equally partially clothed making tea and toast in the kitchen? Worse, with her hair probably resembling a bird's nest, and her face all shiny and devoid of even the tiniest touch of make-up. Even in her wildest dreams—and there had been more than a few where Harry was concerned—she wouldn't have been able to come up with this scenario.

She'd had fantasies, more than she could remember, but they had all featured her perfectly made up and looking ravishing, and Harry suddenly realizing the error of his ways and falling at her feet in adoration before whisking her off to bed. After that, it had been roses round the door and a ring the size of a golf ball.

She sighed. Impossible dreams. Impossible happy-ever-after. Impossible *man*. Still, at least the 'roses round the door' bit was in place. She smiled ruefully. And this was one hundred per cent the sort of house made for a family—babies, children. Harry's babies. She shut her eyes, her heart actually paining her.

Harry had made it clear he would never consider matrimony again, let alone becoming a father. He was now a ruthless bachelor, married to freedom, and only dating women who were happy to embrace their temporary place in his life gracefully. A wife and babies didn't come into the equation anywhere. Perhaps it was a blessing she wasn't his type. If he had fancied her she wouldn't have been able to resist for long, and a brief affair would have left her in a worse emotional mess than she was now.

Hearing his footsteps, she arranged her face into an acceptable expression, even managing a smile as her eyes met his. He was carrying a tray on which reposed two mugs of tea and a large plateful of buttered toast, along with several preserves. 'You have been busy,' she said lightly, thinking how unfair it was that men could look drop-dead gorgeous when they were at their most dishevelled, whereas women merely looked bed-raggled. At least, Harry could. She didn't know about other men, never having spent the night with one.

'Dinner seems a long time ago.' He grinned at her, putting the tray down and gesturing towards the puppy in her lap. 'She's adopted you. Sensible puppy.'

Gina grew hot. It was absolutely stupid to be so affected by the soft warmth in his voice, but she couldn't help it, in spite of knowing this was Harry in flirt mode. It didn't mean anything, not to him at least.

Drawing on the iron self-control that had got her through the last months since that Christmas kiss, she said flatly, 'Hardly sensible. I'm leaving at the weekend for good, and a puppy definitely doesn't feature on my agenda.'

He handed her her tea and offered the plate of toast. She took a triangle, not because she really wanted it, but more to give herself something to do. She had never felt so vulnerable and exposed in all her life.

'You're sure you want to go?' he said after a moment or two had ticked by.

Want to go? She had never wanted anything less. 'Absolutely,' she said firmly. To add weight to her words, she looked him straight in the eye, steeling herself to show no emotion as she said, 'And we had this conversation during dinner.'

He nodded. 'I wasn't convinced then either.'

'I thought I'd made it clear, I need to leave Yorkshire.'

'Ah, but *need* isn't necessarily *want*.' There was a significant little silence as he fixed her with a hard, meaningful look. 'You'll be miserable in London,' he declared authoritatively.

'Thanks a bunch. Some friend you are.' Sarcasm was a great hiding place.

'You told me I wasn't a friend.' His eyes mocked her. 'What exactly am I, Gina? How do you see me?'

She didn't like the way this conversation was going. He was playing games, probably just to kill a few minutes as far as he was concerned.

Fighting for composure, she took a deep breath and lifted her head. She smiled thinly. 'You're my boss's son.'

'*Ex*-boss's son,' he returned drily. 'OK, what else?'

'You're very good at what you do—accomplished, experienced.'

'Thank you,' he said gravely. 'What else?'

'Does there have to be more?'

'I should damn well hope so.' He paused and studied her face. 'As a man,' he said quietly. 'A person. Do you like me?'

'You shouldn't have to ask that, we've worked together for just over a year,' she said weakly.

'My point exactly. And I would have termed us as friends. You, on the other hand, would not. So I'm beginning to realise I don't know how your mind works, which means I perhaps don't know the real Gina at all. In fact, I'm sure I don't. I didn't know you had a lover somewhere in the background, for example.'

His eyes were tight on her, questioning. Rallying herself, and aware she was as taut as piano wire, she said coolly, 'Forgive me, Harry, but I don't remember you discussing your personal life, either. Any part of it. Whereas you know about my family, friends—'

'Not all of them, obviously.'

Ignoring that, she continued, 'My childhood, my youth, my time at university— I've discussed all that—whereas you've been…guarded.'

There was an awkward silence. He stared at her, all amusement gone. 'Yes.' His voice sounded odd. 'I have. I was. But for what it's worth I've never told anyone the full story about Anna before. Apart from my parents at the time I left the country, that is. Does that count for anything?'

She looked down at the toast in her hand. Her heart was a tight ball of cotton wool in her throat, choking her. 'I didn't mean I expected you *should* have necessarily talked to me, just that you can hardly take me to task for the same thing.'

The silence stretched longer this time. 'I appreciate that,' he said at last.

It was still quite dark outside the windows; the rest of the world was fast asleep. It added to the curious sense of unreality which had taken over her. The puppy stirred in her sleep, grunting and snuffling, before becoming quiet as Gina began to stroke her again.

'So you can't be persuaded not to go?'

His voice had been husky, and as Gina raised her head she saw his face was dark, brooding. 'Of course not,' she said bleakly. 'It's not feasible. Everything's been arranged. I've got to move out of my flat Saturday morning; I wouldn't even have anywhere to live.'

'You could use my spare room till you find something else.'

There was something in his eyes that made her feel suddenly light-headed and treacherously weak. Painfully, she said, 'I've got a job in London, a flat. I couldn't let people down. Anyway, the reason I wanted to leave in the first place is unchanged.' It was. It *was*. This sudden interest on his part was all about sex, plain and simple. But it wouldn't be simple where she was concerned. It would be horribly complicated.

'I hadn't been to sleep when I heard you come downstairs,' he said suddenly.

Her throat felt dry. She took a sip of the tea before she could say, 'I was worried I'd woken you.' She was prevaricating; she knew it.

It appeared Harry knew it too. 'Don't you want to know why?'

She couldn't answer, and it was a moment before he said softly, 'It was the thought of you just a couple of doors away.'

'I'm sorry.' Inane, but the best she could do.

'I like you, Gina.'

The atmosphere in the room had changed several times in the last minutes, now it was thick with an electricity that quivered in the air.

She couldn't speak, her only movement her hand on the puppy's silky fur as she continued to stroke it, her eyes fixed on the little body.

'I realised tonight I don't want you to leave Yorkshire.'

Taking all her courage into her hands, she raised her face and looked straight at him. She had to kill this stone-dead, right now. The agonies of mind she'd endured over this man had brought her to the inevitable conclusion that she had to walk away from him, and that had not changed. Sooner or later she'd be old news. The only difference was, if she went sooner rather than later, she would still have her self-respect. 'I don't do one-night stands, Harry,' she said flatly, her pain making her stiff.

'I wasn't talking about a one-night stand.'

'Yes, you were.' She moistened dry lips. 'Perhaps a series of them, but essentially that's all an affair would be to you. You told me yourself, that's all you can offer a woman.'

She saw anger flare in the beautiful grey eyes. 'I don't want the full domestic-scene, admittedly, but that doesn't mean I'm quite the heartless so-and-so you're painting. I'd like to show you that you can find fun and happiness after this guy, if nothing else.'

'How noble.' Suddenly she, too, was furiously angry. 'Thanks, but no thanks.'

'You're not listening to me.'

'Oh, I am.' If the puppy hadn't been in her lap, she would have liked to empty her mug of tea straight over his unfeeling head. 'Believe me, I am. Out of the goodness of your heart, you'll take pity on me long enough to take me to bed a few times. About right?'

His face a picture, Harry said, 'I don't know what's got into you.'

'Into *me*?' He took the biscuit, he really did. 'Harry, if all I was looking for was sex, I could get that anywhere. I'm not quite so desperate, OK? I have to engage my heart and my mind as well as my body.'

'I know that.' He glared at her. 'I know that about you. But we get on, we get on really well in my opinion, and I don't think you find me totally repulsive. Do you?' he added a trifle uncertainly.

It was nearly her undoing. Her fingers holding onto the puppy hard enough for it to raise its head and squeak protestingly, Gina said tightly, 'Harry, I'm sure ninety nine out of a hundred women would take you up on your offer, but I'm the hundredth. Can we leave it at that?'

'You're determined to let this man ruin your life? Force you away from your home and friends, everything you're used to? And don't tell me you want to go, because we both know it isn't like that. You're running away, taking the coward's way out.'

'What about you?' she demanded, her blue eyes flashing. 'Isn't this slightly hypocritical? You've let Anna turn you into someone else, someone you were never meant to be. Oh, you can prattle on about life changing and shaping us and all that waffle when it applies to you; that sounds quite lofty. But, where *I* am concerned, it's ruining my life. Well, let me tell you, Harry, I don't intend to let my life be ruined, but I think yours has been. You've become selfish and shallow, without anything of substance to offer a woman beyond the pleasure of your company in bed. And that wouldn't be enough for me, not by a long chalk.'

She stopped, aware she'd said far more than she had intended. The silence seemed to stretch for ever until Harry finally spoke. 'I take it that's a no, then,' he said acidly.

Her eyes snapped up to his, but she could read nothing in his expressionless gaze. His face had become the bland, smooth mask he adopted at times, a mask she hated. It spoke of withdrawal and control, and it was forged in steel. 'I'm sorry, I shouldn't have expressed myself quite that way, but you shouldn't have pushed me.' Her voice was calm now, but a part of her was dying inside. For it to end like this—it couldn't be worse.

'I see. It's all my fault.' He nodded. 'I had no idea your opinion of me was so low.'

She watched him stretch out a hand for another piece of toast, as though the opinion he'd spoken of mattered not a jot. Slowly she took a sip of her tea. It was cold. Like his heart, she thought, a little hysterically. 'It's an opinion formed from the image you project,' she countered shakily.

He seemed to consider this for a moment, his features in shadow as he leant back in his chair. Gina was glad she could tilt her head and let her hair fall in a curtain as she concentrated on the puppy; the angle of her chair cause the light to fall directly on her, and she needed some help in hiding her turbulent emotions.

After a while, when he remained silent, she sighed inwardly. This was awful. So much was going on in this room that the air was crackling. She'd offended and annoyed him, and she couldn't take this deafening silence one more moment.

She opened her mouth to speak, but he was there a second before her. 'The image isn't all of me,' he said gruffly.

She knew that. The man she loved was a hugely complicated human being. Enigmatic and cold, funny and warm. The sort of man who could slaughter an opponent on the telephone with a few well chosen, crisp words, and yet who would stop to rescue four little breathing pieces of flotsam and jetsam the world had abandoned.

The first time she'd accepted her heart was irrevocably his was when she'd discovered he'd delved into his own pocket to pay the rent arrears of a house one of their ex-employees lived in. The man had a drug problem, and had worked one day in five in the couple of months before Harry had sacked him. When the man's wife had come to the works hoping to find him—and it had transpired he'd been even less at home that he'd been at work and she hadn't seen him for weeks—Harry had taken her home to find three young children were also in the equation. He'd paid the rent arrears, found the woman a job at the works, and arranged for nursery care for the children.

She bit her lip and tried to control the tears that were threatening. 'I didn't think it was,' she said. 'But you have to understand where I'm coming from, Harry. In the matter of love, relationships, togetherness—call it what you will—we're aeons apart. I—I don't want to waste any more time on hopeless liaisons.' That was the truth at least. 'I—I want my heart to be my own again, and I'm the sort of woman who couldn't sleep with anyone, even once, without being involved. It…well it wouldn't be a fun thing for me. At least, it being fun wouldn't be enough without love as well.'

She saw him nod. 'I'd like to know his name, just to be able to tell him what a damn fool he is,' he said so softly she could barely hear him.

Gina gulped. 'I'm a fool as well. I knew what I was getting into but I couldn't find the brake. I don't think I ever will. That's why I need to move away. I don't want to become someone I don't like.'

'You love him very much.'

It was a statement, not a question, but Gina answered anyway. 'Yes, I do.'

'Life's not all it's cut out to be at times, is it?'

It was fine until he'd come along. The puppy had never really settled since she'd half-strangled it, and now it began to squirm with definite intent. 'I'll put her back with her sisters.' She stood up, aware of him following her as she walked through to the utility room.

Outside the window, the first pink streaks of dawn were beginning to creep into a charcoal sky, and the dawn chorus was in full song. It was going to be another beautiful spring day.

After depositing her charge with the other sleeping puppies, Gina left the utility room and walked through to the kitchen where Harry was waiting for her. 'We might get in an hour's kip before the alarm goes,' he said, half-smiling. 'Or they wake up.'

She tried to match his easy manner. 'I don't have an alarm.'

'I'll bang on your door, don't worry.'

When they reached the landing, he paused with her outside her room, his voice soft as he said, 'I didn't want to hurt you, Gina.'

'What?' For an awful minute she thought he had guessed.

'By rubbing salt in the wound about this guy.'

Her limbs turning fluid, she managed to say fairly coherently, 'You didn't,' as relief flooded her.

'And you're not a coward. Far from it.'

She had leant against the wall when he'd first spoken, needing its support, and he'd propped one arm over her head, his fingers splayed next to her hair. She was aware of the faint lemony smell of shower gel, the same make as she had found in her *ensuite*, presumably, but mixed with Harry's body chemicals it was altogether more spicy, sexier. Summoning brain power from some deep reserve, she murmured, 'Leaving is more an act of self-survival, Harry.'

He nodded. 'I'm beginning to understand that. And if you need a friend, any time, any place, call me, OK? I'll be there.'

He wasn't a man to offer empty platitudes. Touched and very near to bursting into tears, she didn't dare to attempt to speak. Instead she leaned forward on tiptoe and kissed him swiftly on his cheek.

She heard his quickly indrawn breath, but he remained quite still as she slipped under his arm and opened her bedroom door. It was only when it was shut that she let out her breath, her heart pounding.

She stood frozen inside the room, her ears straining to hear any sound from the landing, but it was absolutely silent. After some minutes she walked over to her bed, the tears streaming down her face, but her mind too weary to struggle with the reason why. With the robe still intact she pulled the duvet over her, shutting her eyes as the tears continued to seep under the lids.

She fell asleep within a minute, her face damp and salty, and her body and mind utterly spent.

CHAPTER SIX

HARRY stood for some time on the landing, shaken to the core. Which was crazy, he told himself vehemently once his racing heart had begun to steady. It had hardly been a kiss, for crying out loud. And Gina had been quite unmoved, sailing into her room and shutting the door as though she hadn't just turned his world upside down.

No. No, it hadn't been.

Yes, it had.

He groaned softly, raking the hair out of his eyes with an unsteady hand and padding to his own room at the far end of the shadowed landing. Once inside he began to pace the floor, his brows drawn together in a ferocious scowl.

What the hell had happened out there? And downstairs; why had he asked her to stay around when he'd promised himself that was the last thing he'd do? What would he have done if she'd agreed to his ridiculous proposal? And it *was* ridiculous, however you looked at it. She was besotted by some bozo who had messed her around for months, if not years, and she was leaving him because she didn't want a no-strings-attached relationship.

So what did he do? Harry asked himself grimly. He offered

her the same sort of deal. No wonder she'd looked at him as if he was mad.

He walked over to the window, looking down at the sleeping garden where the first blackbird was singing its heart out, and then raised his eyes to the pink-streaked sky. The dawn of a new day. In the aftermath of his breakup with Anna, his mother had told him she viewed each dawn as the start of the rest of her life. The past, with all its regrets and mistakes, was gone and unalterable, the present and the future were virgin territory to make of what you would. He'd appreciated she'd been trying to help, but he'd been so full of anger and bitterness he'd dismissed her ideology as coming from one who had never really had anything to contend with. He had been arrogant then. He was still arrogant, perhaps. Gina would say there was no 'perhaps' about it.

Smiling darkly, he turned from the window and looked over the room. When he had bought the house he'd had it re-decorated throughout before he had moved in, and his room and *en suite* were a mixture of dark and light coffee-and-cream. No frills, no fuss, but luxurious, from the huge, soft billowy bed to the massive plasma TV and integrated hi-fi system. Everything just the way he liked it. His *life* was the way he liked it.

Harry dragged his hand over his face. Or it had been, up until twelve months ago, when he had walked into his father's office and a blue-eyed, red-haired girl had given him the sweetest smile he'd ever seen. Twelve months. Twelve months of disturbing thoughts and dreams, of dating women he didn't want to date but who would provide a distraction and give his body some relief.

He shook his head, beginning to pace again. Put like that,

it sounded mercenary, even seedy. He'd used those other women, he couldn't deny it. But they'd been happy enough with his conditions, he reasoned in the next breath.

But with Gina there could be no conditions. He caught his breath, stopping dead and groaning softly. He'd known all along she was a till-death-do-us-part woman. What he hadn't allowed for was that he would find it so hard to let her slip out of his life, or that she was desperately in love with another man. His arrogance again. He grimaced sourly. He'd taken her completely for granted, he supposed.

No suppose about it. The retort was so loud in his head, it was as though someone else had spoken it.

He hadn't even considered she was involved with someone. She had always chattered with him so openly he'd felt he knew all about her, from cradle to present day. And all the time there had been another man in the background. Someone she'd laughed and talked and slept with. His stomach muscles clenched.

Was he jealous?

You bet your sweet life he was. And, however he tried to dress it up as anger at this guy who had taken her heart and then carelessly broken it, it was more the picture of them in bed together he couldn't take.

So if—*if*—she'd let him provide a shoulder to cry on, what would that mean? Suppose—*just* suppose—it led to more. It wouldn't be right to assume she could cope with yet further goodbyes. Would it?

No, he knew damn well it wouldn't. His stomach muscles unclenched, but only to turn over in a sick somersault. He'd be taking a darn sight more than he was ready to give. He had been young and idealistic when he'd got involved with Anna;

that was his only excuse for the gigantic mess that had ensued. He only had to shut his eyes to recall the trapped helplessness he'd felt then, the overwhelming panic and despair.

But Gina wasn't Anna. In the twelve months he'd known her, she'd been sweet and funny, serious and determined, honest—painfully so at times, at least where he was concerned—and forthright. But never, *never* manipulative. And 'cruel' wasn't in her vocabulary. She was also as sexy as hell without even knowing it. He'd seen work on the factory floor slow right down when she'd walked through, and some of those guys had had their tongues hanging out.

Using the sort of expletive that would have shocked even the most worldly veteran, Harry thumped his fist into the palm of his hand. He had to get a handle on how he was feeling. Confusion wasn't an option here. Perhaps that was the answer—feeling like this was turning him into someone he didn't recognise, so the obvious, the practical thing to do was to let her walk away and then get on with his life. Out of sight, out of mind. It had worked with all the others since Anna.

Something inside twisted, and he answered the feeling with an irritable growl deep in his throat. Enough. He needed some fresh air to clear his head. You couldn't beat straight-forward logic, and it hadn't let him down in the past. Outside, with no distractions, he could *think*.

He took a deep breath and tried to relax, glancing at his watch. Another couple of hours before he needed to wake her and get going. He had to get himself sorted and back on track in that time.

He pulled on some clothes without bothering to shower first, leaving the room swiftly and making his way downstairs on silent feet. Once in the garden, he paused. His original intention had been to go for a walk, but sitting out here would do as well.

Breathing in the sharp, scented air, he walked to a wooden bench set at an angle to the dry-stone wall that surrounded the grounds. From there he had a perfect view of the house, which slumbered in the early-morning light. Somewhere close by a wood pigeon was cooing, a little rustle at the base of the wall telling him the tiny harvest mice he'd noticed a few times running up and down the old stone were about. No doubt there were myriad nests deep in the crevices, where generations of the enchantingly pretty creatures had been born. This whole place—the house, the garden, the surrounding countryside— spoke of permanence, he realised suddenly. Subconsciously, had that been one of the reasons which had attracted him to the property when he'd first seen it?

He frowned, not liking the idea. It didn't fit into how he saw himself. Like everything else that had happened in the last twenty-four hours, it was acutely disturbing, in fact.

Gradually his revolving thoughts began to slow down as the peace of his surroundings took over. The sky lightened still more, garden birds beginning the job of hunting for breakfast, and the flock of sparrows that had residence in the privet hedge separating the swimming pool and tennis court from the rest of the garden squabbled raucously as they went about their business.

It was cold; he could see his breath fanning in a white cloud in front of him when he breathed out. But still he sat on in the burgeoning morning, his mind clearer than it had been for a long, long time.

He loved her. He'd loved her for months, but had been too damn stubborn to admit it to himself because it was the last thing he'd wanted or needed in his life. And now the laugh was on him, because even if he had declared himself she would have told him—gently and kindly, because that was Gina's way—she was in love with someone else. Height of irony.

It was over an hour later that he rose to his feet, and with measured footsteps went into the house.

GET FREE BOOKS and FREE GIFTS
WHEN YOU PLAY THE...

7 7 7

Lucky 7

SLOT MACHINE GAME!

Just scratch off the silver box with a coin. Then check below to see the gifts you get!

YES! I have scratched off the silver box. Please send me the 2 free Harlequin Presents® books and 2 free gifts (gifts are worth about $10) for which I qualify. I understand I am under no obligation to purchase any books, as explained on the back of this card.

306 HDL ESJT   ## 106 HDL ESM5

FIRST NAME	LAST NAME

ADDRESS

APT.#   CITY

STATE/ PROV.   ZIP/POSTAL CODE

7	**7**	**7**	Worth **TWO FREE BOOKS** plus 2 **BONUS** Mystery Gifts!
🍒	🍒	🍒	Worth **TWO FREE BOOKS!**
♣	♣	♣	Worth **ONE FREE BOOK!**
🔔	🔔	🍒	**TRY AGAIN!**

www.eHarlequin.com

(H-P-07/08)

Offer limited to one per household and not valid to current subscribers of Harlequin Presents® books.

Your Privacy - Harlequin Books is committed to protecting your privacy. Our Privacy Policy is available online at www.eHarlequin.com or upon request from the Reader Service. From time to time we make our lists of customers available to reputable third parties who may have a product or service of interest to you. If you would prefer for us not to share your name and address, please check here ☐.

The Harlequin Reader Service — Here's how it works:

Accepting your 2 free books and 2 free mystery gifts places you under no obligation to buy anything. You may keep the books and gifts and return the shipping statement marked "cancel". If you do not cancel, about a month later we'll send you 6 additional books and bill you just $4.05 each in the U.S. or $4.74 each in Canada, plus 25¢ shipping & handling per book and applicable taxes if any.* That's the complete price and — compared to cover prices of $4.75 each in the U.S. and $5.75 each in Canada — it's quite a bargain! You may cancel at any time, but if you choose to continue, every month we'll send you 6 more books, which you may either purchase at the discount price or return to us and cancel your subscription.

*Terms and prices subject to change without notice. Sales tax applicable in N.Y. Canadian residents will be charged applicable provincial taxes and GST. All orders subject to approval. Credit or debit balances in a customer's account(s) may be offset by any other outstanding balance owed by or to the customer. Please allow 4 to 6 weeks for delivery. Offer available while quantities last.

If offer card is missing write to: Harlequin Reader Service, 3010 Walden Ave., P.O. Box 1867, Buffalo NY 14240-1867

BUSINESS REPLY MAIL

FIRST-CLASS MAIL   PERMIT NO. 717   BUFFALO, NY

POSTAGE WILL BE PAID BY ADDRESSEE

HARLEQUIN READER SERVICE
3010 WALDEN AVE
PO BOX 1867
BUFFALO NY 14240-9952

NO POSTAGE
NECESSARY
IF MAILED
IN THE
UNITED STATES

CHAPTER SEVEN

WHEN Gina awoke from an extremely decadent and satisfying dream featuring her, Harry and a bowl of whipped-chocolate ice-cream, it was to bright sunlight. She stretched as she opened heavy eyes, and then realised what had woken her as another knock sounded at the bedroom door: Harry's alarm call.

Her voice husky with a mixture of sleep and remembered passion, she called, 'It's OK, I'm awake,' and then squeaked with surprise with the door opened and Harry strode in carrying a tray.

He seemed unaware that she'd hastily dragged the duvet up to her chin, owing to the fact the robe had worked itself open and under her back, smiling as he said, 'I didn't know if you're a tea or coffee girl, so I brought both.'

Her voice higher-pitched than usual, Gina said, 'Either, thanks, but you needn't have bothered.'

'No bother.'

He placed the tray on the bedside cabinet and gazed at her from the advantage of being bright-eyed and bushy-tailed. He was very big and very dark in the pastel-coloured room, and his sheer magnetism detracted from the realisation that he wasn't dressed in his normal suit and tie for a moment or two. When she could get her breath, Gina said carefully, 'Are we taking the puppies and then coming back here?' as she took in his black jeans and casual blue shirt.

He didn't answer this directly. With a smile that turned the grey eyes smoky-warm, he said, 'Drink your "either" and then come downstairs when you're ready. There's no rush.'

She stared at him. Something was different. Or was it just the casual clothes? Still clutching the duvet to her chest with one hand for all the world like a Victorian maiden, she brushed the hair out of her eyes with the other. 'What time is it?'

He glanced at the gold watch on his wrist. 'Eleven o'clock,' he said calmly.

'Eleven o'clock?' She struggled into a sitting position, which wasn't easy with the robe and the need to remain decent hampering her. 'It can't be. What about work?'

'You don't work, or at least not till Monday.'

'I mean *you*.'

'I decided to give work a miss today.'

'You've never given work a miss in all the time I've known you,' she said, astounded.

'Then perhaps it's high time I did.'

'What about your father? And Susan? She's still settling in, and—'

'Will be fine. She's that sort of woman,' he said quietly.

Well, that was true at least. Unable to take in that half the day had gone already, Gina stared up at him. His eyes were dark, unblinking, as they watched her; his slightly uneven mouth curved in a wry smile that told her her bewilderment was plain on her face. She hoped her bout of crying the night before didn't show in pink-rimmed eyes. Gathering her wits, she swallowed hard. 'Are the puppies all right? You haven't taken them already, have you?'

'The puppies are fine,' he said soothingly. 'I had them out on the lawn for half an hour earlier. That was hectic,' he added drily. 'They can shoot off like exocet missiles when they want to.'

She wished she didn't love him so much. Controlling her voice with some difficulty, Gina forced a smile as she said, 'You should have woken me earlier to help.'

'You needed your sleep.'

What did that mean—that the bags under her eyes could carry potatoes, or was he just being thoughtful? Deciding it was probably better she didn't know, Gina wondered how long he was going to continue standing watching her. 'Have you phoned the animal sanctuary?'

'No,' he said calmly.

She waited for him to elaborate and, when he didn't, began to feel acutely uncomfortable. It was all right for him standing there, fully clothed and showered and shaved. She felt like something the cat wouldn't bother to drag in.

His open-necked shirt showed the springy black hair of his chest, and his jeans were tight across the hips. The flagrant masculinity that was such a part of his attraction was even stronger today, and more than a little intimidating. Her mouth dry and her heart racing, she decided to take the bull by the horns. 'I'll see you downstairs in a little while, shall I?' she said pointedly.

'Violet-blue.'

'Sorry?'

'Your eyes are the colour of the wild violets that grow close to the stone wall in my garden,' he said very softly. 'Beautiful little flowers, tiny but exquisite. Much better than the cultivated variety.'

'Oh.' The sudden tightness in her chest made her voice a little husky when she said, 'Thank you.'

'My pleasure.'

He didn't seem in any hurry to go. 'I'll be down shortly and we can take the puppies straight away, if you like. I know you must have things to do, and I need to get home and sort out the last of my things.' Now he *had* to take the hint.

He gave her a long look. 'I'm cooking a bacon flan and baked potatoes for lunch, or perhaps I should say brunch.' His reproachful voice expressed disappointment at her ingratitude.

'Are you?'

He seemed surprised by her astonishment. 'Of course. You didn't think I'd send you home without feeding you, surely?'

He made her sound like a stray dog that had landed on his doorstep—four of which were already occupying his utility room. 'I just thought you'd want the puppies off your hands as soon as possible,' Gina said carefully, wondering when he'd become so touchy.

His frown smoothed to a quizzical ruffle that did the strangest things to her breathing. 'Oh, I see. So you're not in a mad rush to get away, then?'

'Considering it's eleven o'clock in the morning, if I was I've failed miserably, wouldn't you say?' Gina said a little tartly.

He smiled. 'You didn't have anyone calling round first thing, I hope?'

She thought about Janice in the flat below. Until this very moment she had forgotten she'd promised to cook Janice breakfast before she went on her shift at the local hospital, where she worked as a nurse. It was to have been a goodbye-and-we'll-keep-in-touch meal and, because of the shift Janice was on this month, breakfast had been the most appropriate time. Blow and double blow. She hated to let people down. The trouble was when she was in Harry's company the rest of the world faded into the background. 'I did, actually.' She felt awful now. 'But I can put that right later.'

A thick black eyebrow lifted. 'I'm sorry.'

He didn't sound sorry. In fact for some reason he seemed put out, if the look on his face was anything to go by. 'It doesn't matter.' *Just go, go.*

Harry didn't go. His mouth had thinned, accentuating its uneven curve, and his gaze was hard when he said, 'It never pays to let someone walk all over you, you know.'

She stared at him. 'No, I suppose it doesn't,' she agreed bewilderedly.

'And a clean break should be just that—a clean break.'

Had she missed something here? 'I'm sorry, Harry, but I don't follow.'

'It was him, this guy who's effectively told you thanks but no thanks, who was calling round, wasn't it? Hell, can't you see him for what he is, Gina? He knows how you feel about him and why you're leaving, and yet he calls round to...what? Why was he calling round?'

Gina tried not to gape. For a moment her brain whirled, and then she forced her face into an indignant expression. 'A friend of mine who lives in the flat below, a *female* friend, was coming for breakfast,' she said haughtily. 'OK? So, whatever your overactive little mind has come up with, it's wrong.'

It took a second or two for the outrage to be replaced by a sheepish expression that immediately melted Gina's heart— not that she would have revealed it for all the tea in China. 'Sorry,' he said. 'I put two and two together and made—'

'Going on a hundred? Yes, that much was perfectly clear.' She ought to be furious at the assumption she was giving house room—or, perhaps more accurately, bedroom—to her supposed lover. But his concern for her—and she didn't flatter herself it was anything but the *friendly* concern he'd spoken of before—warmed her aching heart. Harry had had lots of women in his life, he didn't try to pretend otherwise, but she doubted if he would have been so genuinely solicitous for the females who flitted in and out of his bed at regular intervals. And he certainly wouldn't have referred to them as friends. Perhaps she ought to be grateful for small mercies? She was distinct and different to the rest, in some small way, at least.

'I jumped to an erroneous conclusion, and I should have known better.'

He could do the gracious-apology thing really well, Gina thought, as she watched a slow smile spread over his handsome face.

'You're not the sort of woman to have second thoughts once you've made up your mind about something, or to say one thing and mean another.'

Oh boy, little did he know. 'Quite,' she said firmly.

'I'll leave you to get dressed,' he said with silky gentleness. 'Brunch will be ready in about twenty minutes.'

When the door closed behind him, Gina continued to lie in complete immobility for another moment or two. Then she flung back the duvet, swinging her legs out of bed and wrapping the robe back round her, before padding to the bathroom. There she scrutinised herself in the mirror and groaned softly. Dark smudges under eyes that definitely bore evidence of the weeping of the night before. And her hair! Why did her hair always decide to party during the night? At uni she'd shared with girls who'd gone to bed sleek and immaculate, and woken up sleep and immaculate. Or, at the most, slightly tousled.

Fifteen minutes later the mirror told her she'd transformed herself into someone who wouldn't frighten little children.

She had washed her hair and rubbed it as dry as she could before bundling it into a high ponytail at the back of her head. The essentials she always took to work in her bag—moisturiser, mascara, eye-shadow and lip gloss—had done their work and made her feel human again. Just.

She'd had the foresight to wash her panties through before going to bed and drape them over the radiator in her room—she did so hope Harry hadn't noticed the skimpy piece of black lace—and, armed with the knowledge she was clean and fresh, she took a deep breath and opened the bedroom door.

Brunch with Harry. The last meal she would ever eat with him, she thought a trifle dramatically, but without making any apology for it. She *felt* dramatic. In fact she felt a whole host of emotions surging in her breast, none of which were uplifting.

Once downstairs she paused in the hall. Sunlight was slanting in through the window on to the ancient floorboards, causing a timelessness that was enchanting. The whole cottage was enchanting. She could imagine what it would be like in the height of summer, with the outside of the house engulfed in roses and honeysuckle and jasmine. Violet dusks, the fragrance of burning leaves drifting in the warm air, dark-velvet skies pierced with stars, and overall a sense of whispering stillness. Did he sit on the verandah on such evenings, a glass of wine in his hand and his eyes wandering over the shadows, sombre and broodingly alone?

The image wrenched her heart and she mentally shook herself. It was far more likely the current blonde would be sitting on his lap or as near to him as she could get, no doubt anticipating the night ahead with some relish, she told herself caustically. And who could blame her?

A slight movement at the end of the hall brought her head swinging to see Harry standing watching her. 'I thought we'd eat in the breakfast room, OK? It's less formal than the dining room, but a bit more comfortable than perching at the breakfast bar in the kitchen.'

Gina nodded, quickly arranging her face into a smile as she walked towards him. 'Can I do anything to help?'

'Carry the salad through? I'll bring the other dishes.'

The breakfast room was situated off the kitchen and was quite small but charming, with wooden shutters at the leaded windows, and an old, gnarled table and chairs in the centre of the room. The only other furniture consisted of an equally old dresser on which brightly blue-and-red-patterned crockery sat, a bowl of flowering hyacinths on the deepset window sill filling the room with their sweet perfume.

After looking in on the puppies, who were all sound asleep, Gina seated herself as Harry said, 'Red or white wine? Or there's sparkling mineral water or orange-and-mango juice, if you'd prefer?'

'Fizzy water, please.'

She watched him as he poured her a glass, and then one for himself, after which he served her a portion of the flan and she helped herself to a baked potato and some salad.

The breakfast room was cosy, too cosy. Gina hadn't reckoned on them sitting so close. There was a small nick on the hard, square jaw where he'd cut himself shaving, and her body registered it with every cell. Clearing her throat, she looked at her plate as she said, 'This—this looks lovely, Harry.'

'Thank you,' he said gravely.

'Did—did you make the flan yourself?' *For goodness' sake, stop stammering. What's the matter with you, girl?* She wanted to close her eyes and sink through the floor.

He nodded lazily, taking a sip of his drink before he said, 'I told you, I like cooking. There are those who've said they haven't lived until they've tasted my chunky borsch.'

She glanced at him to see if he was joking, but he appeared perfectly serious. Taking him at face value, she said primly, 'I'm sorry, but I don't know what that is.'

'No?'

He grinned at her, his eyes warm, and his mouth doing the uneven thing that always turned her insides to melted marshmallow. She was used to banter with Harry, mild flirting and harmless innuendo. It was part of office life, and meant nothing. It was altogether different when sitting at his table in cosy intimacy. 'No,' she said flatly, her voice at odds with the army of butterflies in her stomach.

'Well, I make mine with smoky bacon and red peppers and celery, so it has a sweet-and-sour flavour. You put cabbage, potato, bacon, tomatoes, carrots, onion and a few other things in a pan and simmer for forty minutes or so before adding beetroot, sugar and vinegar and simmering some more. Serve with fresh herbs and soured cream.'

His eyes had focused on her mouth as he had been speaking, and something in their smoky depths brought warm colour to Gina's cheeks. She'd never have dreamt talking cookery could be so sexy.

'It's a nice dish on cold winter evenings, curled up in front of a log fire. You ought to try it some time.'

She swallowed. Curled up on a rug in front of a roaring fire with Harry would be food enough. 'I don't think my new life in London will feature many log fires.'

'Shame. You seem a chunky-borsch-and-log-fire girl to me.

Her eyebrows lifted on a careful inhalation. Play the game, she told herself. Keep it casual and funny. 'I'll just have to make do with caviar and glitzy nightclubs instead,' she said lightly. 'As befits a city girl.'

He regarded her across the table, but she couldn't read what was going on behind the grey eyes. 'Nope, don't see it,' he said at last. 'Sorry.'

'You don't think there'll be men queueing to buy me caviar and champagne and take me to all the best places?' she asked with mock annoyance.

'I didn't say that.'

Suddenly in the space of a heartbeat the atmosphere had tightened and shifted; there was no teasing in his voice or eyes now, but only an intent kind of urgency which took her aback.

He leaned forward, his face close and his eyes glinting. 'There'll be men, Gina. Plenty, I should think. But I don't think they will be what you need.'

She couldn't drag her eyes from his, and the moment hung between them like an unanswered question, but it was a question she'd never ask. It might open up something she would never be able to handle, she told herself frantically. This was just Harry being Harry. She was here, available and perhaps he fancied a change from his usual diet of cool, slender blondes. He didn't have, and would never have, any interest in an ongoing relationship, probably not even in a lengthy fling. He'd made that perfectly clear yesterday, when he'd confided in her about Anna and his disastrous marriage.

Better to have loved and lost than never have loved at all? The little voice in her head was probing, insistent.

Not in this case. If she gave herself to him it would be heart, mind, soul and body, and when he walked away she'd never recover from it. Especially if it ended badly.

Forcing her gaze down to her plate again, she picked up her fork, hoping he wouldn't notice the shakiness in her voice when she said, 'I'll just have to take each day as it comes, I guess.'

There was a pause, as though he was weighing his next words. She waited with a kind of breathless urgency while pretending to enjoy the flan.

When he said, 'Including this one?' she breathed out twice before lifting her eyes.

'Meaning?' she asked quietly, amazed she could sound so cool when there was an inferno inside.

'I need your help.'

'Oh?' She nodded. 'To take the puppies to the sanctuary? I've already said I'll come with you.' The inferno was out, deluged by stark reality. He was a rich, intelligent and hugely gorgeous man. Of course he wasn't interested in her.

'Not exactly.' Another brief pause. 'I've decided to keep them.'

'What?' She genuinely thought she'd misheard him. He couldn't possibly have said what she thought he had said.

'The puppies, I'm going to keep them.' He ate a large chunk of flan with every appearance of enjoyment. 'I already rang Mrs Rothman this morning to tell her she needn't come in today because I was going to be around, and I asked her if she'd be prepared to extend her days from Monday to Friday, essentially to be here from ten to four each day, to take care of them for the large part of the time I'm away.'

'And she said yes?'

'On the proviso she could bring her own dogs any time her husband isn't able to be home.'

'But—'

'What?'

'Well, I hate to coin a phrase, but dogs are for life, not just for Christmas. You talked of travelling some more, moving abroad, no—no responsibilities.' She stared at him, utterly in shock. This wasn't the Harry she knew. 'You can't have them for a while and then dump them at some sanctuary or other in a year or two. That wouldn't be fair. And *four* of them!'

Her voice had risen the more she'd spoken, and now she was aware of Harry settling back in his chair and surveying her over the top of his glass. 'You don't think much of me, do you?' he drawled mildly.

If you only knew, she thought for the second time that morning.

'I don't intend to dump them, as you so graphically put it. Not in a year or two, not ever. The poor little scraps have gone down that road once, and once is enough for any poor mutt. I've decided to take them on, and that means for life. OK?'

Not OK. *So* not OK. Feeling the world had shifted on its axis, Gina tried again. 'Harry, travelling or moving to another country is one thing, but something else entirely with four dogs in tow.'

'I do actually know that.'

She ignored the edge to his voice. 'I don't think you do.'

'I've decided to stay put, Gina.'

'What?' She blinked.

Her astonishment caused his anger to vanish like smoke, and now he grinned. 'Don't know me as well as you think you do, eh?' There was immense satisfaction in his voice. 'It's not just a woman's prerogative to change her mind. I've decided I'd go a long way before I found another house like this one, and it suits me. England suits me.'

'But you said—'

'Excuse me,' he interrupted mildly, 'But wasn't it you who was saying this house was a beautiful empty shell?'

Her eyes met his. *Touché*, she thought with a mixture of irritation and gratification. Irritation that he always had an answer for everything, and gratification that her words had obviously registered. 'I wasn't recommending that you fill it with a pack of dogs.'

'And I probably wouldn't have considered it myself right at this moment in time, but for fate taking a hand,' he admitted. 'But the grounds are extensive, they say dogs are the best burglar deterrent there is, and I rather like the idea of keeping the four of them together after all that's happened. I'll give Mrs Rothman a hefty pay rise for the extra work they'll involve until they're house-trained and so on, and with her ever-increasing brood of grandchildren the money will come in handy.'

Gina bit her lip. This was ridiculous. 'Keep one or perhaps two, if you must,' she said slowly, unable to believe he could have had such a radical change of heart regarding the future and his plans to travel. 'But not all of them.'

'Why not?'

She couldn't very well say she didn't believe him when he'd spoken of staying put. 'Four times the amount of mess and trouble?' she prevaricated.

'Four times the amount of fun and pleasure.'

She frowned. 'Four times the amount of squabbling and barking?'

'Four times the amount of canine love.'

He waited for her to continue, one dark brow raised. Gina mentally conceded defeat. It was true the dogs would have a wonderful life here, with the huge garden and each other—doggy paradise—but... 'Dogs shouldn't be left alone all day.'

'I thought I'd explained, they won't be,' he said with elaborate patience. 'Weekends I'm home, I might even arrange things so I work from home some mornings, and Mrs Rothman will be around for most of the time I'm out.' He seemed amused. 'I thought you'd congratulate me for taking some responsibility after your scathing words yesterday.'

'They weren't scathing.' She averted her gaze to the hyacinths. She supposed they *had* been.

'No? I'd hate to be in the firing line if you really get the bit between your teeth, then.'

She should never have agreed to stay the night, Gina told herself miserably, every nerve in her body as tight as piano wire at the closeness of him. 'Harry, you must do as you please,' she said quietly after a few moments had ticked by. 'This is nothing to do with me.'

'I guess not,' Harry said levelly. 'It's just that I've an appointment with the local vet this afternoon. I want him to look the puppies over and start their inoculations, if he thinks they're old enough. I was going to ask you to stay long enough to help me with them. I thought you might help me choose some bedding, leads, collars, that sort of thing, and of course I need to pick up some food and so on.'

She stared at him, feeling slightly hysterical. Today was supposed to have been spent clearing out the flat of the last bits and pieces, ready to spring-clean it from top to bottom before the new occupants took over on Saturday. She'd arranged to leave work on Wednesday evening so she had two clear days to sort everything out. Now that was already severely curtailed, and he was asking her for more of her time. This was utterly unreasonable and the whole situation was surreal. Harry didn't *do* permanence, dependability and personal responsibility, not where other people—or, rather, females—were concerned. But then these weren't people, they were dogs.

'Eat your food.' His voice came quiet and steady. 'I'll take you home after lunch. I shouldn't have asked.'

No, he shouldn't. And she shouldn't be considering his request for one second. She swallowed, her tongue stumbling over her words as she said, 'Are you absolutely sure you want to keep them? Have you really considered what you're taking on? It'll mean twelve, thirteen years of commitment, maybe longer. Have you really changed your mind so completely from yesterday, Harry? I...I need to know.'

He looked back at her, and she was aware that a tiny detached part of her mind was thinking that the hard angles of his chiselled face and body made him look older than his thirty-three years. But then he had the sort of bone structure that was ageless; at fifty, sixty, he'd still probably give the impression of being in his forties.

He reached across and took her hand as though he had the perfect right to touch her, and she had to remind herself the gesture was an expression of the easy friendship he felt for her as a sharp tingle shot up her arm with the power of an electric shock. 'I can understand your scepticism,' he said softly, 'But I mean every word, Gina. Perhaps there's been a part of me hankering for a more settled existence for some time, I'm not sure, but our conversation yesterday, finding the puppies...' He shrugged. 'Something gelled over the last twenty-four hours. They'll be company.'

She wondered how she could retrieve her hand without it being a big deal, and decided she couldn't. The trouble was, loving Harry as she did, *wanting* him, made any physical contact acutely painful in an exhilarating, pulsing kind of way. Stiffening her spine, she aimed to look at him levelly, face expressionless. 'So you're saying you intend to be around for some good time?' Even more reason for her to get away, then. 'Have you had a change of heart about taking over the firm too, when the time comes? Your father would like that.'

'Whoa, there.' He smiled, leaning back and letting go of her hand. She felt the loss in every pore. 'I didn't say that. To be truthful, I don't see myself in Dad's role, I never have. We're two very different people. I'd like to steer towards business consultancy, something which will enable me to decide where and when I work. That way, if I want a few weeks off at any time, it's no big deal. I pick and choose.'

Gina stared at him doubtfully. 'Could you afford to do that? And would enough people want you?'

His eyes were deep pools of laughter. 'If I had a problem with the size of my ego you'd be the perfect antidote. But, in answer to your question, I have enough contacts to succeed.'

Independent to the last. Nothing had changed, not really. He might have decided to establish some kind of base in his life but he was still a free spirit, not willing to be answerable to anyone, even in his work life.

Smothering her anguish with difficulty, Gina nodded. 'Lucky you,' she said as nonchalantly as she could manage. 'It sounds the perfect scenario.'

'I think so,' he agreed. Taking another large bite of the flan, he chewed and swallowed before saying, 'What do you think of my cooking expertise, then?'

Surmising he'd had enough intense conversation for one day, she tried to match his lightness. 'Marks out of ten?' She tilted her head, as though considering. 'Eight, nine, perhaps.'

'Not the full quota?' he asked in mock disappointment. 'I can see you're a very hard lady to impress.'

'Absolutely.' A shaft of sunlight was touching the ebony hair, slanting across the hard, tanned face and picking out the blue-and-red pattern on the plates. She wondered how you could love someone so much you ached and trembled with it and yet it didn't show. 'But you've won regarding the pooches. I'll help this afternoon. For their sake, though,' she added with what she thought was admirable casualness. 'Not yours.'

She'd expected some laughing words of thanks, or a teasing remark, along the lines that he knew she wouldn't hold out against him *and* the puppies. Instead, his eyes stroking over her face, he said gently, 'Thank you, Gina. You're a very special lady.'

Don't. Don't do tender. She could cope with almost anything else but that. The lump in her throat prevented speech, and she wasn't going to risk her luck by trying to force the words past it. Instead she compromised with a bright smile.

It seemed to satisfy him, if the warmth in his eyes was anything to go by. Feeling as though she was swimming against the tide and liable to drown at any moment, she applied herself to the food on her plate, even though each mouthful could have been sawdust for all the impact it made on her taste buds.

CHAPTER EIGHT

When Gina and Harry left the house a couple of hours later the puppies were contained in a large robust pet-carrier Mrs Rothman had popped round just as they'd been finishing lunch. Snuggled on one of Harry's jumpers on top of a layer of newspapers, they seemed perfectly happy gazing out of the wire front as they travelled to the veterinary surgery, apparently suffering no bad memories of their fateful car trip the day before.

After a thorough examination the vet pronounced them fit and well, but declined to start their inoculation process for another two weeks. He also wryly wished Harry good luck.

Gina and Harry came back armed with a mountain of feeding and drinking bowls, pet beds, rubber toys, puppy collars, leads, brushes, combs and special puppy-feed, and once home the utility room quickly resembled a pet shop. Gina stood, gazing around at all the paraphernalia, unaware her thoughts were mirrored on her face until Harry said drily, 'No, I haven't taken on more than I can handle.'

'I didn't say a word.'

'You didn't have to.' He smiled. 'I'm a big boy, Gina, or hadn't you noticed?'

She'd noticed all right. If anyone had noticed, she had.

'And I'm more than capable of taking care of this little lot. I shall build a temporary pen in the garden for when they're outdoors, like the vet suggested, and put some strategies in place, OK?' He gestured at the book the vet had recommended—*Your Dog from Puppyhood To Old Age*—and which they had bought on the way home. 'And I'll read that from cover to cover tonight.'

His enthusiasm melted her. Realising it was imperative she maintained her cool facade, she nodded. 'Good, you'll have to. And I hope Mrs Rothman's pay rise is going to be a huge one.'

He grinned. 'Massive. Now, what are we going to call them?' he asked cheerfully. 'Any ideas?'

'Call them?' *We?*

'You had as much to do with their rescue as I did. I'd like you to choose their names.'

'I couldn't.' How could something so simple cause such pain? 'They're your dogs, Harry.'

'And I'd like you to name them. Women are so much better at these sorts of things than men. I'm getting into the mental habit of referring to them as One, Two, Three and Four, and that's no good. Don't worry—I shan't turn up in London with them in my arms, demanding you make an honest man out of me for the sake of the babies,' he added, his grin widening. 'You're only naming them.'

Not funny. She laughed obligingly, hating him and loving him in equal measure. He could talk about her being so far away with total unconcern now, apparently. Bully for him. Well, she could show she didn't give a hoot either. 'Well, it's spring,' she said slowly. 'How about flower names? Daisy for the little one, Rosie for the biggest, and perhaps Poppy and Pansy for the middle two.'

Harry eyed her in horror. 'If you think I'm standing in the middle of a field shouting Pansy you've got another think coming,' he said bluntly.

'OK, perhaps not Pansy, then. How about Petunia?'

'I don't think so, for the same reason.'

'Primrose?'

'You've already got Rosie.'

'Iris?'

'The name of my mother's best friend. She might take it personally.'

'Violet?' Gina was getting desperate.

'Mrs Rothman's christian name. I'd rather keep her on side, if you don't mind.'

'Oh, I don't know.' She glared at him. 'I've named three out of the four, the last one you'll have to think of.'

'OK.' He stood leaning against the wall, watching her with unfathomable grey eyes.

His hair had been slightly ruffled by the spring breeze outside, and his black-leather jacket was slung over his shoulder. He looked good enough to eat.

'I'll take you home now, if you're ready,' he said calmly.

It felt like a slap in the face. Somehow, and she wasn't sure from where, Gina found the strength to nod casually and smile.

She said goodbye to the puppies—who were curled up fast asleep in a heap in the corner, worn out by their afternoon excursion—as though her heart wasn't breaking, and then fetched her handbag and jacket. It felt like the end of the world as they walked out to the car, and she was vitally aware of Harry whistling under his breath. Silently calling him every name she could think of, she smiled her thanks and slid gracefully into the car when he opened the passenger door.

The late afternoon was one of bright, crisp sunlight and bird song, but already the shadows of evening were beginning to encroach across the garden. She'd get nothing done today, Gina thought as she watched Harry. Not that that mattered. Nothing mattered. This was the last time she was going to see him, and the swine didn't give a damn. He was whistling. He was actually *whistling*.

Harry didn't say much on the drive back, and for this Gina was thankful. She would have found it terribly difficult to make polite conversation the way she was feeling.

When they drew up outside the house in which her flat was situated, she was out of the car before he had even left his seat, saying, 'No, please don't get out,' when he opened the driver's door. 'You need to get back to the puppies.'

'A minute or two will make no difference.' He walked round the bonnet, handing her the satellite-navigation system the folk had bought her as he said, 'You'll need this, won't you?'

Forcing a smile, she took the box. 'Definitely. Well, I'd better get cracking on cleaning the flat. Goodbye, Harry.'

His eyes narrowed, glittering in the gathering twilight. 'I thought you were going to let me have your new address.'

As if you really care. Hurt causing a constriction in her chest that made it difficult to breathe, Gina nodded. 'Of course,' she lied flatly. 'I'll phone it through tomorrow, if that's all right? I've got your mobile number.'

'Thanks for all you've done over the last twenty-four hours,' he said very softly. 'I appreciate it.'

Of course you do. I fell in with what you asked me to do, like the weak fool I am where you're concerned. What's not to appreciate? 'It was nothing. Glad to help.' *Please go. Go before*

I break down completely or grab hold of you and can't let go.
Something that was becoming more likely with each moment.

He still didn't move. 'I'll let you know how the puppies get on,' he said pleasantly.

'Thank you.'

'You must come and see them when you're next up visiting your parents.'

'Yes.'

'By then I'll have sorted out a name worthy of her sisters for Number Four.'

Gina nodded.

Whether her lack of enthusiasm got through to him she didn't know, but he studied her face for a long moment as she stood perfectly still and tense. 'I must let you go, I've delayed you long enough.'

You could delay me for ever if I thought I had the slightest chance of meaning anything to you. She knew she ought to say something light and casual, something which meant they would part on easy, friendly terms, but words were beyond her. The ache inside overpowering, she made to turn away just as he bent and lowered his mouth to hers.

She froze. His lips were warm and firm, and it was no brief peck but more a caressing exploration that deepened moment by moment. Utterly captivated, she couldn't have moved away if her life had depended on it, but she fought responding to his kiss with every fibre of her being, knowing once she did she would be lost. He thought she was in love with someone else, but if she kissed him back in the way she wanted to it might set that intimidatingly intelligent mind thinking.

Grasping the box in her hands so tight her knuckles were shiny white, she told herself over and over again to remain absolutely impassive, but it was no good. This was Harry and he was kissing her. As her mouth began to open beneath his, she told herself she didn't want to think or reason, she wanted to *feel*. In thirty-six hours she would be gone for good, and this would have to last her a lifetime. What did self-respect and dignity matter compared to that?

It was the box in her hands that saved her, preventing her from throwing her arms round his neck and pressing against him as she wanted to. As it made its presence felt by digging into her chest, he became aware of it too, straightening and smiling a faintly rueful smile as he said, 'Sorry.'

The blood thundering in her ears, she couldn't match his cool aplomb. Hoping the trembling inside wasn't visible to those intent grey eyes, she lowered her flushed face, her voice a murmur as she said, 'I have to go, Harry.'

'I know.' A moment passed, then another. 'Goodbye, Gina.'

'Goodbye.' This time she did turn from him, walking towards the front of the house by instinct rather than sight, her eyes dry but unseeing.

It took enormous self-will to turn after she had opened the front door to the house and wave, but somehow she did it. She was aware of his arm lifting in response, and then she almost fell into the hall, shutting the front door and leaning against it as her heart beat a violent tattoo.

How long she stood there after she heard his car start and then draw away she didn't know, a mixture of crushing regret and sheer undiluted dread at never seeing him again turning her into a frozen statue. He had gone. Nothing she had experienced in her life thus far had prepared her for this moment, for desolation so consuming she could taste it.

Eventually she made her way to her flat on leaden feet, her

head thudding. She felt physically sick. Opening the door, she walked in, carefully placing the box on the small table in the tiny square of hall before continuing into the sitting room. It was all exactly as she had left it the morning before, several cardboard boxes half-filled with this and that standing on the carpet, and the loose cream covers of her two two-seater sofas in a pile on the coffee table waiting to be ironed. The young couple who were renting the flat after her had made her an offer for her furniture, and she had been glad to accept it, the flat in London being already furnished.

Numbly she walked across to the big picture-window and looked out over the river and rolling fields beyond. This view had thrilled her soul when she had first found the place; it still did, normally. This evening she felt as though nothing would ever touch that inner place wherein lay joy and happiness and everything good ever again.

As though in an effort to prove her wrong, the sky slowly began to flood with colour as the twilight deepened. A blaze of deep scarlet and gold turned the evening shadows into vibrant mauve and burnt-orange, all nature conspiring to put on a breathtaking display. All Gina could think of was Harry. She pictured him returning home in the quiet of the scented evening, the peacefulness of the old thatched cottage, the puppies scrambling to meet him when he walked into the utility room.

It was worse now she had seen where he lived, this constant stream of images in her mind. How was she going to escape them? How was she ever going to live the rest of her life with this leaden emptiness weighing her down? And why couldn't she cry? She had expected to cry when the last goodbye was over.

Eventually the sunset was blanketed by darkness, a

crescent moon hanging in the velvety blackness surrounded by tiny, twinkling stars.

Her legs stiff with standing in one position for so long, Gina roused herself to walk through to the kitchen where she made herself a cup of coffee before checking her answer machine. Two somewhat plaintive messages from her mother, reminding her she was due to have dinner with them the next evening, one from Margaret, checking up on how she was on leaving work, and another from Janice, wondering where she'd got to that morning. The last two had also come through as text messages on her mobile, but she hadn't replied to them, partly because it would have been difficult to explain she had gone home from work with Harry and stayed the night. Some things were best said face to face, or at least voice to voice.

She rolled her shoulders, attempting to stretch the tension from her neck. Considering she'd only had a few hours' sleep in the last twenty-four hours, and that the nights before last hadn't been particularly good either as she'd gnawed at the prospect of leaving Yorkshire and Harry until the early hours, she didn't feel particularly tired. Odd, light-headed, numb, but not tired.

One long hot bath, and two aspirin for the headache drumming at her brain later, Gina sat in her pyjamas, staring at a TV programme she had no interest in as she sipped at another cup of coffee. She forced herself to eat two chocolate biscuits, a separate segment of her brain expressing amazement she could quite easily stop at two rather than half a packet, as was normal.

The telephone rang at eleven o'clock, but she made no attempt to answer it, not wanting to talk to anyone. After the answer machine had delivered the perky message she'd thought so funny when she'd first recorded it, Harry's voice said quietly, 'You're probably asleep by now, but I just wanted you to know I've thought of a name for the puppy, and it *is* one I could yell in the middle of a field. Zinnia. What do you think? My gardening book tells me it's a plant of the daisy family with showy rayed flowers of deep red and gold, like your hair. I thought it appropriate.'

There was a pause, and Gina found she wasn't breathing.

'Oh, and the book also said in the language of flowers it means "thoughts of absent friends",' he finished even more softly. 'Goodnight, Gina. Sleep well.'

Sleep well? You've made me a mental and emotional wreck, and you calmly say 'sleep well'? And talking about her hair, and naming the puppy in memory of absent friends! All nice and chatty and 'I don't give a damn', while she was in pieces here. The anger that suddenly consumed her was so strong it was palpable.

He was a heartless so-and-so, that was what he was. She began to pace the room in her rage. Keeping everyone at a distance, pushing them away, not caring how many hearts he broke along the way.

No, that wasn't quite true. She stopped for a moment before beginning to pace again. He had his affairs with women who knew the score; it wasn't his fault she'd fallen in love with him so irrevocably. And one thing was for certain: if he'd had the faintest idea of how she felt, he'd have run a mile. She'd only got the invite to his home because he'd thought she regarded him as a friend. She smiled bitterly. Friend!

After a few minutes she took control of herself and played back the message again. This time there was no anger, but Harry's voice released the dam of tears that had been building all day. She cried until there were no more tears left and her face was a mess, whereupon she walked into the kitchen and made herself another coffee. She stood staring at it, and then very purposefully walked across to the sink and tipped it away.

She needed milky cocoa to help her sleep, she told herself firmly. And perhaps a couple of slices of buttered toast too. Her heart might be in shreds, she might be looking at an empty future devoid of husband and children and all the things she'd thought she'd have one day, but she wasn't going to crumble into tiny pieces now or at any other time. She wouldn't let herself. And she wasn't going to let this sour her either, not if she could help it.

The cocoa and toast helped. As she ate, she felt she was becoming herself again rather than the desperate, partly unhinged creature she'd felt since walking in the door earlier.

After finishing her supper, she washed the mug and plate and put them away. Tomorrow they would be packed with all her other bits and pieces, ready to be transported to her new life.

She didn't want to go. She bit hard on her lip as tears threatened again. But she would. Not for ever; she realised that now. But maybe for a year or two, long enough to come to terms with the fact that Harry would never be hers. She just couldn't do that here. All the time she would be hoping, hoping. It had sapped her strength over the last months, turned her into someone she didn't want to be.

But she would come back home. Not to this flat, or to Breedon & Son, not even to this town where she'd been born and grown up. But somewhere close. She wasn't a city girl and she never would be. The country was in her blood, in her veins and bones: swelling moorlands, wooded valleys where rivers wind over ageless stones and rocks, empty moors with the curlews crying and swooping; that was her. She had been born into a land of wide expanse, of pure summer air heavy with the sweetness of warm grass, and winter winds so cold they could take your breath away. She would never be happy for long hemmed in by buildings and concrete.

Straightening her shoulders, she walked out of the kitchen and into her pretty gold-and-white bathroom. She brushed her teeth thoroughly, refusing to dwell on the reflection of pink-rimmed swollen eyes in the mirror, eyes that held an expression that actually pained her. She didn't want to look like the lost, sad girl in the mirror.

Once in bed Gina lay quietly in the darkness, her arms behind her head. She was doing the right thing. She was doing what she had to do, it was as simple as that.

Within a few minutes she was fast asleep.

CHAPTER NINE

HARRY sat watching the glowing embers in the grate. The fire had burned low, sending flickering shadows across the room, and the puppies had long since gone to sleep, the four of them ignoring their individual beds and all curling up together in one. He smiled as he recalled the plump tangle of paws and tummies and tails, before his face took on the brooding expression it had worn for the last hour or two.

Who was this man who had captivated Gina? And 'captivated' wasn't too strong a word. It couldn't be anyone at work; he'd have noticed. More to the point, so would the die-hard gossips in two minutes flat. Nothing escaped them. No, it was no one at Breedon's, so it had to be someone she'd met elsewhere. A neighbour? Someone she'd perhaps grown up with and then noticed when she'd come back from university? It happened like that sometimes. How long had she been with him?

He stretched his long legs, glancing at his watch, and then reaching for the glass of brandy at the side of him. Taking a swallow, he let the neat alcohol burn a path down his throat into his stomach before replacing the glass on the table by his chair.

She hadn't been living with him. Had that been her decision or his, bearing in mind the man's reluctance to put a ring on her finger? When he thought about it, she'd really told him very little, just the bare facts without the slightest embellishment. Which wasn't like Gina.

Or was it? He blew out a sigh, then scrubbed his hands over his face. He was blowed if he knew any more. He thought he'd got her all taped, but he couldn't have been more wrong. Which proved—if nothing else—that women were a different species. Not that he'd had any doubts about that in the first place.

Gina had said she didn't think he liked women much, and he'd admitted to being cynical. The truth of the matter was that for the last decade he'd been guided by fear, plain and simple. Although it hadn't been plain to him, and it had been anything but simple. But fear was what had controlled him, galling though it was to concede the truth. He had believed falling in love again would strip him naked, and nothing was worth that.

The fire crackled and spat as an ember fell inwards in a shower of sparks, and Harry shivered although the room was warm.

And so for years he'd had his cake and eaten it too—up to a point. But everything had to be paid for. He hadn't realised the sort of man he had become until she had pointed it out in her warm, soft voice. And then the genie had been out of the bottle and there'd been no going back. He had had to face the feelings which had steadily grown and matured over the last twelve months. Gina. Oh, Gina. And all the time there'd been a shadowy figure in the background he hadn't had the slightest idea about.

Needles of jealousy pierced him, and he found himself struggling against the emotional vulnerability. Just as he had always known, love didn't play fair.

The temptation to wallow in his own self-pity was strong, and for a few minutes he indulged himself. Then he raised his head, finishing off the remaining brandy and standing to his feet.

OK, so he had missed the love boat where Gina was concerned. He had to deal with that and get on with life. She liked him; he still believed there was a kind of spark between them, and if her heart hadn't been elsewhere who knew how things would have developed? But since she had told him about this man she had made it very clear she wasn't in the running for anything from him beyond friendship. He could scarcely argue with that. Even in the friendship stakes the ball was in her court. He had asked her for her new address in London more than once. If she wanted to give it, she would. If not...

He placed the fireguard in front of the grate, but after straightening stood gazing, unseeing, into the dying embers. Anna had made a fool of him in more ways than one. Tricking him into marriage, lying to him, laughing about it with her friends, and then the constant threat of taking her own life. And all in the name of love, a love that had taken him for every penny he'd had in the divorce settlement whilst painting him as the worst sort of villain. To cap it all, she'd married again within the year. Some love.

But, if he was honest, once the exhaustion and pain and anger had receded, it was the humiliation that had hurt the most. Shame that he had ever been fooled so completely, that people had been laughing at him behind his back. The degradation had bit deep, and he hadn't known how to handle it except by running away. Not the most noble or impressive episode of his life. His mouth twisted. He'd been confused, shamefaced, scared—all those things a man wasn't supposed to be. And, although time had brought logic and reason to bear, he only had to shut his eyes to recall the panic he'd felt as his life had spiralled out of his control.

What would she make of his phone message when she heard it in the morning? She would know what he was really saying, of course, but at least this way he would save them both the embarrassment of her having to reiterate her love for this man. But it would keep the door open for her to contact him in the future if she came to a point where she put this guy behind her.

Damn it. He moved irritably, shaking his head. He was rusty in the twists and turns of the love game. Taking what he wanted when he wanted it had been so much simpler.

He walked quietly through to the utility room to check on the puppies before he went upstairs. It was still hard to determine which head went with which body in the heap of gently snoring canines. Had he decided to keep them purely to show Gina he was prepared to take on responsibility and commitment—a sprat to catch a mackerel?

No. The answer was a relief, and he realised the question had been at the back of his mind all day. Convincing Gina he'd been talking a load of rubbish before had been part of it, certainly, but he wanted—he *needed*—them for himself. They were the beginning of a new phase of his life, whether Gina played a part in it or not. He was tired of his shallow love-resistant life plan. Sure, it had meant an existence free from pain and emotional doubts and worry, but of late it had left a nasty taste in his mouth.

He was sick of coming home to an immaculate silent house, of autonomy. Maybe the kick start to all this had been the shock of his father's heart attack, when he'd realised for the first time that his parents were mortal, that one day they wouldn't be around. Certainly there had been no question of staying in the States and continuing to do his own thing when his father had needed him so badly. And then he had met Gina.

Maybe the last decade he had been screwed up. Or maybe he had just been working through issues that had had to have their time. Whatever. He shrugged. That time was gone, and he didn't believe in harping back or castigating himself with regrets about a past he couldn't change.

Right now, what would once have been stifling and terrifying had become satisfying, and all the maybes he'd been chewing over boiled down to that. He had been slowly changing the last year without knowing it, and although the realisation had come as a hell of a shock, now he thought about it, it hadn't been a sudden process. Loving Gina hadn't been a sudden process but a quiet, steady growth of something incredible. *She* was incredible. And she was walking out of his life in twenty-four hours, and there wasn't a damn thing he could do about it.

He closed his eyes for an infinitesimal moment and then turned and walked upstairs, wondering which of the gods of fate and destiny were having a good laugh at his expense.

CHAPTER TEN

WHEN Gina emerged from a troubled restless sleep early on Saturday morning, the big black cloud which had hovered over her constantly the day before was still firmly *in situ*.

All Friday she had cleaned and scrubbed and sorted, only stopping to answer the telephone—Bryony and Margaret had called, along with a work colleague and two friends—and make herself some lunch. She'd fed Janice breakfast first thing, thereby fulfilling her obligations of the day before, and then had gone to see her parents for dinner as arranged. She'd been bright and cheerful throughout. It had nearly killed her.

Rolling over onto her back, she stared at the cream-painted ceiling. This was it. D-Day. She was packed and sorted, all she needed to do this morning was to strip the bed and give the bathroom one last, quick clean after she had showered and washed her hair.

Outside her reliable little car was bulging at the seams with her belongings. The young couple who were taking over the flat were due to arrive at eleven o'clock with the letting agent who handled things for the landlord. He'd called by yesterday to inspect the place, and had expressed himself more than satisfied with its décor. So, everything going like clockwork, then.

Gina sat up in bed, brushing a strand of hair out of her eyes. *He hadn't phoned back yesterday.* She looked towards the window where weak sunlight was struggling to break through the soft muslin curtains. But then, why would he?

Swinging her legs out of bed, she stared miserably at the carpet. She didn't doubt for a moment that out of sight meant out of mind with Harry. It had been stupid to imagine—to *hope*—he would call. But then that was it with Harry, she couldn't *help* hoping. Which was exactly why she had to leave. And she would *not* call him, not now, not ever. This had to be a once-and-for-all solution to what had become a gigantic problem, a clean, swift finale.

When the telephone rang she reached out for it automatically. The only person who would ring at this time in the morning was her mother. Her father had been very positive about the move to London, or at least he'd pretended to be, which was all that mattered. On the other hand her mother had been in a state last night, and had cried when she had left their house. Anyone would have thought she was emigrating to Australia, rather than taking up residence in London for a while, she thought wryly, steeling herself for more reasons why it was ridiculous if she left Yorkshire as she said, 'Hello, Mum,' into the receiver.

There was a moment of silence. 'Sorry, this isn't Mum.'

She was glad she was sitting down. Unfortunately she couldn't say a word, though.

'Gina? It's Harry. I know it's early, but I wasn't sure what time you were planning to leave.'

Respond. Say something. Squeak. Anything. 'I—not yet. I mean—' Her throat started to tighten but she pushed past it. 'I'm still in bed.'

'I've woken you. I'm sorry.'

She didn't disabuse him. Let him think her stuttering and stammering was due to being woken up. 'It's all right,' she managed fairly coherently, her heart hammering so hard it actually hurt. 'Is anything the matter?'

'The matter?'

She might sound odd, but he didn't sound much better. A sudden thought struck. 'The puppies, is anything wrong?'

'What? Oh no, they're fine.' She heard him clear his throat. 'Look, I didn't thank you properly for all you did the night we found them, staying like you did and then helping the next day.'

'Of course you did.' She glanced at her wrist where the gold watch gleamed in the dim light. She had slept with it on, needing the link with him. Her throat tightened still more.

'I don't think so. Anyway, I thought it might be nice if we had breakfast together on your last morning in Yorkshire. That's if you haven't other plans?'

He definitely sounded odd. Easing the air past her constricted throat, she closed her eyes. It would be madness to see him this morning. Crazy to invite more pain. And for what? An hour of his company, maybe two if she was lucky. It would knock her sideways again, she knew it. The sensible thing, the *only* thing, was to make an excuse.

The silence seemed to stretch for ever. Then Harry said, 'Gina? Are you there?'

'Yes.' Her voice was calm, but part of her was screaming inside. She was such a fool where this man was concerned. 'And breakfast would be lovely.'

'Good. I know a great café not far from where you live.'

He sounded really pleased; she wished she could see his face. Gathering her wits, she said, 'What time will you be here?'

Another silence. Then he said, 'Actually I'm sitting in my car outside your house. I watched the sun come up.'

Her train of thought crashed. 'Why?' she asked stupidly.

'Couldn't sleep.'

He was here, outside? She fell backwards on the bed, her hair fanning around her on the cream duvet like flames. Her legs dangled off the edge as she stared upwards. 'I shall need to have a shower,' she mumbled helplessly.

'Fine, take as long as you want, there's no rush.'

'I've got to hand over the keys at eleven.'

'You'll be back in plenty of time, don't worry.'

'Do you want to come and wait up here?' she asked reluctantly, wondering if he was forever destined to see her looking as though she'd been dragged through a hedge backwards. Oh, for sleek, manageable hair that didn't require dampening down every morning.

He must have sensed her unwillingness. 'No, I'm fine where I am, listening to the radio. Did you know it's going to be another beautiful day once the morning mist clears? Cold but sunny, the forecast says.'

It was going to be the most beautiful day in the world because she would see him again one last time—and also the worst, because she was going to have to say goodbye all over again. But he had thought enough of her to come. She hugged the fact to her. OK, it might be because he'd had a bad night and couldn't sleep, but it was *her* house he'd ended up at. 'How long do you have before you have to get home and see to the puppies?'

'Mrs Rothman's taking care of them. I've been around the last forty-eight hours, so she agreed to change her days and come over the weekend. Relax, Gina.' His voice held a touch of amusement now. 'I haven't absolved myself of all responsibility so soon.'

'I didn't think you had,' she said, hurt he could think so. 'I'll be down shortly.'

A quick shower later, and with her hair bundled into a high ponytail on top of her head, she dressed in the jeans and top she had laid out the night before. They weren't the best clothes for the last meeting with the man she loved; she'd have preferred to leave him with a picture of something far sexier. But they were certainly appropriate for breakfast in a café.

As she pulled on her light jacket, she stopped suddenly. Her body was zingingly alive and on full alert, her heart pumping like a piston engine. She groaned softly. In every other area of her life she was a grown woman with complete control over her emotions; Harry was her Achilles heel. Just look at her. She'd woken up this morning feeling like the world had ended, and now she was—

What was she? She paused, considering. Daft. Stupid. Utterly crazy. Still, hey, no one was perfect.

He wasn't sitting in his car when she emerged from the house, but was standing leaning against it, gazing out over the river with his back towards her. She felt her breath catch in her throat as she took in the big dark figure clothed in jeans and a black-leather jacket. The rush of love that swamped her was so powerful that for a moment it blinded her. And then her vision cleared and he was still standing there, ebony hair shining in the sunlight, and the faintly brooding quality that was habitual with him more marked in the fresh spring morning.

He turned as she walked towards him, his handsome face breaking into a smile that warmed her aching heart. 'Hi.' The smoky voice caressed her nerve endings. 'You were quicker than I expected.'

'Good. I don't like to be predictable.'

'Predictable?' He shook his head. 'Not you.'

She liked that. It made her feel more in control, even slightly racy. Of course she knew it wasn't true, but that didn't matter. 'Where are we going exactly?' she asked as she reached him.

'Exactly?' His head tilted, teasing her. 'A couple of miles away to a somewhat infamous lorry-driver's café I found by chance one morning months ago. It's slightly off the beaten track, but always full. Apparently the lorry drivers' grapevine highly recommends it, and that's all the advertising the place needs.'

'Infamous?' she questioned doubtfully.

'Well, perhaps not infamous. Just a little basic, and populated by characters who look more suited to some weird cult-movie half the time, but the food's great and it's clean. OK?' His smile widened. 'It's all right, Gina. You'll be perfectly safe with me. I wouldn't let anything happen to you.'

A light reply hovered on her lips, but it was never voiced. It was the way he was looking at her. She couldn't quite fathom what was in his eyes, but it increased the ache in her heart a hundredfold.

Then he opened the car door for her and the earth began to spin again.

Once he joined her in the car her senses picked up on the faint scent of aftershave on fresh male skin. She shivered.

'Cold?' He'd noticed, immediately starting the engine and turning up the heating. 'You'll soon warm up.'

Oh yes. Her body was always in danger of internally combusting around Harry. 'This is nice,' she said with a casual-ness she was extremely proud of. 'An impromptu breakfast.'

'I'm glad you think so.' He pulled out of the parking space in front of the house, glancing at her little car as he did so. 'Sure there's enough room for you in there?' he asked mildly. 'I'm not sure it's safe to drive packed to the hilt like that.'

She brindled immediately. 'Of course it is.'

'Gina, you're supposed to be able to see out of the back window.'

'I need to get my stuff to London, don't I?'

'So why don't I take some of it for you and follow you down?' he suggested nonchalantly.

'You?' She stared at the dark profile, utterly taken aback. 'No, no, it's OK.' The last thing she wanted was to start her new life with Harry a step or two behind her. 'Loads of people have offered to help, but I prefer to do this myself.'

'Loads of people?' The odd note in his voice was back.

'My parents, my sisters…'

'Right.' He paused and then said slowly, 'Do you mind if I ask you something on the personal side?'

Her stomach fluttered. 'No,' she said warily. 'Ask away.'

'This guy you've been seeing—is this move to London a definite conclusion to all that? What I mean is—' he paused again, checking both ways before pulling on to the main road '—is there any chance he'll be able to wheedle his way back into your life if he comes begging and pleading?'

'He won't,' she said faintly.

'But if he did?' Harry persisted. 'Look, what I'm really asking is whether you want to move on. Start dating again.'

Gina knew her eyes had widened. She nervously moistened her lips, utterly out of her depth, and every nerve in her body sensitized and pulsing. Why did he always have to have such a *physical* effect on her? It didn't help. Swallowing hard, she said, 'I don't know,' because he was waiting for an answer and she had to say something.

Then she knew what it was to have her heart jump into her throat as he pulled the car off the main thoroughfare and into a minor road where he immediately parked on the grass verge. His eyes were so dark they were almost black as he turned to her, his voice throaty as he said, 'He's not the be all and end all, Gina, whatever you think now. I can prove it to you.'

She was mesmerized as he bent his head and took her lips, one arm sliding round her shoulders and his other hand cupping her chin. It was a deep kiss, long and warm and without reserve, and she was helpless before the flood of desire racing through her. Her hands were resting on his chest, and the warmth and scent of him was engulfing her, the hard, strong beat of his heart beneath her fingers.

His lips left hers, moving over her cheek to her ear, then her temple, the tip of her nose and back to her mouth. Her lips parted to allow him greater access, and he took the vanquished ground with a low growl in his throat, kissing her until there was no past and no present, just the two of them in a world of touch and taste and smell.

When he finally released her and drew back she couldn't move or speak for a moment, every ounce of her will fighting to regain control over her composure. She watched him rake a hand through his hair before he said, 'I'd like us to start seeing each other, Gina. We can take it as slow as you want, but you can't deny there's something between us.'

She drew in a ragged breath. Now he wasn't touching her,

she had to try and *think*. She stared at him, trying to take in what had just happened and—more importantly—what he'd said.

Something between us. What did that mean? Sexual attraction on his part—more than she'd ever dreamt or hoped for, admittedly—but now…not enough. Not loving him as she did. If this encounter had happened when he had first come back to England, then she might have been able to convince herself that with time and patience on her part he could learn to love her. But this wasn't a romantic movie where the guy suddenly realized what he'd wanted all his life was right under his nose with the girl next door.

This was real life. This was Harry. He might have decided to allow four very small dogs into his life, but that was vastly different to changing his mind about happy-ever-after. He avoided entanglements like the plague.

Slowly, she said, 'I'm going to London, Harry. It wouldn't be realistic to think we could date, surely?' She hoped the trembling in her body wasn't reflected in her voice.

'I don't see why not.' He still had one arm resting across the back of her seat, and as he shifted slightly every part of her registered the action. 'It's hardly the end of the world.'

'But—'

'What?' he asked softly.

'Why now?' She knew her cheeks were firing up, but still she ploughed on. 'I mean, we've known each other for over twelve months, and you've never—' She stopped. 'Never asked me out,' she finished awkwardly.

He surveyed her under half-closed lids. 'Perhaps I don't believe in mixing work and pleasure.'

Pleasure. The word trickled along her nerve endings like warm, silky honey. Warning herself not to falter, she said quietly, 'I'm sorry, but I don't buy that. Be truthful. You've never noticed me in that way before. So I ask again, why now?' She studied his face, trying to find a clue in the chiseled features as to how he was really feeling.

He smiled, but this time it didn't reach his eyes. 'You're wrong, Gina. I noticed you in *that* way, as you put it, the first moment of the first morning.'

She couldn't say anything, she was stunned by his admission. A brief thought of all the days and nights of agony she had endured thinking he could never—would never—see her as a desirable woman darkened her eyes, but then he was speaking again.

'As to the reason why I never asked you out, that kiss might have had something to do with it,' he said cryptically.

She stared at him, confused. 'I'm sorry but I don't understand.'

'I knew that if we got together it would mean something.' The keen eyes were tight on her face.

Feeling as though she was wading through treacle, Gina made a huge effort to clear her whirling mind. This was probably the most important conversation she would have in her life, and she had to remain calm and focused. 'And that was bad?'

'Oh yes,' he said with a sardonic twist of the lips. 'Then. I wasn't ready. I needed to work some things through in my head. But now circumstances have changed. *I've* changed. And when you said your relationship with the other guy was over...'

Suddenly, with the force of a blow in the solar plexus, she understood. He thought she was in love with someone else, someone she was leaving Yorkshire to forget. She was moving to London where she'd be finding her feet for a while. He fancied her, but he hadn't wanted any close involvement or complications, and so he'd done nothing about it. *Now it was all different.* He could indulge in a long-distance affair, which would of necessity mean it was much less intense, her being at one end of the country and him at the other. Secure in the knowledge she loved someone else, he could pop down to London now and again for the odd bit of sex—perhaps even convincing himself he was doing her a favour. The poor little country girl all alone in the big city.

Gina took a deep breath. 'Let me get this straight,' she said, with a composure born of silent fury. 'You're suggesting we start dating, even though I'm in London and you're up here. Right?'

He nodded. 'Motorways made short work of distance these days.'

True, but distance could also be a very pliable tool in the hands of someone dedicated to non-commitment as he was. 'And how often would these…dates occur?'

'That would be up to you,' he said quietly. 'Of course, with you wanting to get away from here, I'd be prepared to come to you.'

How magnanimous. That way the ball would always be entirely in his court. If he thought she was getting a little clingy at some time in the future, curtail the visits. In the past she had often wondered if love and hate were equally powerful emotions. Now she knew.

Gina thought of screaming at him that he was the most insensitive, selfish man since the beginning of time. That she would rather die than become his little weekend diversion. That he could take his cold heart and stuff it where the sun didn't shine. But she had come this far—to the last minute of the last hour, metaphorically speaking—without losing her dignity, and without him guessing how she felt about him, and all the pain of the last twelve months had to be worth something. She turned and looked out of her side window while she fought for control. Then, turning back to face him, she arched an eyebrow, keeping her voice pleasant when she said, 'I'm sorry, Harry, but it wouldn't work.'

'I disagree.'

I just bet you do. Trying to ignore the breadth of his shoulders and the way a muscle had clenched in the hard male jaw—always a sign with Harry he wasn't prepared to take no for an answer—she forced a smile, although it nearly killed her. 'I'm sorry,' she said again, 'But for me it wouldn't.'

'Because of this guy?'

Although his eyes were hooded and his face was betraying nothing she sensed there was an awful lot going on behind the expressionless façade. Resentment that she hadn't got down on her knees and thanked him for his so generous offer? Pique at her imaginary lover who had cheated him out of what he'd seen as a very nice, no-strings-attached little set-up? Irritability that she couldn't see the sense of such a logical arrangement?

Inclining her head, Gina said, 'Partly because of him, yes. I'm afraid I'm not the sort of girl to go to bed with one man when I'm thinking about another.'

She had thought the implied insult would be enough to put him off but she should have known his tenacity was stronger. 'I never imagined you were. How far and how swiftly our relationship would develop would be entirely up to you. Contrary to what you obviously think, it *is* in my capacity to wine and dine a woman without insisting on the evening ending in bed.'

Believe me, you wouldn't have to insist. And that was the trouble. She wouldn't be able to resist him on the first date, let alone the second, and then where would she be? Counting the hours till the next time he phoned or came to see her? Driving herself crazy imagining him with someone else when he wasn't with her? Fearing every time he left it would be the last time, that he'd finally got tired of her? The previous year had told her she was in danger of becoming someone she didn't like because of how she felt about him; if she allowed herself to become little more than his clandestine affair tucked out of sight in London, the last of her self-esteem would be gone.

She knew she could be as tenacious as him, especially when emotional suicide was the alternative. She shrugged carefully. 'I guess the bottom line is that I don't want any links to Yorkshire, Harry. It's as simple as that. I want—I *need*—this to be a clean break if it's going to work. And it has to work.' Horrified, she heard the catch of a sob in the last words, and prayed he hadn't heard it too.

He had. His voice husky, he said, 'I didn't want to upset you, Gina.'

Upset me? You've taken my heart and I can never have it back for anyone else. She shook her head blindly. 'You haven't. I'm fine.'

'I could wring his neck.' He lifted a hand and traced the outline of her lips, his eyes stormy with an emotion she couldn't put a name to.

For a moment she didn't grasp what he meant and then she sighed, her skin burning where he had touched. How had all this come about? This time last week she would have thought the events of the last forty-eight hours impossible, and yet they'd happened. She'd seen his home, *slept* in his home, got

to know him even better, and now this...breathtakingly frightening proposal. Frightening, because every cell in her body
was urging her to say yes and to hell with the consequences.
Breathtaking, because the thought of making love with him
would be all she ever asked of life.

A strange feeling came over her. For a moment it was as
though she had stepped out of her skin and was watching the
pair of them from outside the car. She could have times like
this—of being with him, sharing part of his life—if she agreed
to start seeing him. They would be a couple, if only to a point.
But she would be in his life. And, when it finished—and it
would finish—there would be memories to linger over down
the years, recollections of shared meals, laughter, *love*. Love
on her part, at least. It would be something. Surely it would
be something, whereas now she had nothing.

She stared at him, her lips already forming the words that
would take her down a path she'd sworn just minutes before
she wouldn't walk down, when he said, 'You need to eat. Hell,
I need to eat.' And he turned from her, starting the engine in
the same movement.

For a second she felt sheer, undiluted panic that she had
lost the moment. Her heartbeat in her throat, she felt anger
and helplessness and a hundred other emotions besides, but
then he was turning the car in a semi-circle and they'd snaked
onto the main road again.

After a few moments she glanced at Harry out of the corner
of her eye. Tight lines of tension radiated from his grim
mouth, and his rugged good looks could have been set in
stone. Clenching her hands together in her lap, in a small voice
she said, 'I'm sorry, Harry.'

'Three "I'm sorry"s in the space of as many minutes are

two too many between friends.' He glanced at her for one swift moment, but the hard countenance had mellowed. 'Besides which, you have nothing to be sorry for. It's too soon, I should have known that. Damn it, you haven't even left yet.'

She didn't want to leave. Ask me again and I'll stay. Don't be understanding and considerate, not at this late stage.

'We're going to have breakfast, and then I'll take you home so you can see to the last-minute bits and pieces, OK?'

She nodded, sunk in misery.

And then he surprised her, reaching out and taking one of her hands and holding it tight as he said, 'Don't look so tragic; that wasn't the point of the exercise, believe it or not. It might be somewhat ungallant to say it, but I don't usually have such an adverse effect on women.'

He was trying to lighten the moment, but it only increased her pain. That and the feel of his warm flesh holding hers. She wanted him so badly she could taste it. He had offered himself—something of himself anyway—and she had turned him down. What was the matter with her? So what if he couldn't do roses round the door and happy-ever-after, at least he'd been honest about it. How many men sweet-talked a woman into bed with promises of for ever and then did a runner? Hundreds, thousands, every day of every week, worldwide. She would have given everything she possessed to hear him say what he'd just said a few months ago, even as little as a week ago.

But something had changed irrevocably in the last three days. It had started the moment she had walked out of Breedon & Son with him and had continued ever since.

It had to be all or nothing. OK, most women would say she was mad, but there would be at least one who understood. She loved him too much to compromise. In the long run, it really was as simple as that. And it sucked, because she was going to end up with nothing.

She felt as though her mind was a pendulum, swinging from one extreme to the other.

He only held her hand for a moment or two, but the feel of him remained much longer, and when they drew up outside a strange ramshackle building tucked away in a tree-bordered lay-by her body was still burning. She glanced at the sprawling one-storey building, which was mostly of wood, a few tables and chairs scattered haphazardly outside.

'I told you it wasn't lace doilies and china cups,' said Harry, grinning, his mouth lifted in an appealing curve that made her want to kiss the corner of it.

'I think the word you used was infamous.'

'Ah, yes. Well, come and see what you think. We don't have to eat outside, by the way, there's plenty of room in the café.'

Gina felt a little apprehensive as they walked into the café. She saw immediately that, although it appeared spotlessly clean, everything appeared to be on its last legs. The tables and chairs were basic to say the least, and quite a few appeared to have been mended with odd scraps of wood. The wooden floor was horribly scuffed and marked, and there were oilcloths on the tables rather than linen tablecloths. A small wiry man with an incredibly lined face and shock of grey hair hailed Harry immediately. 'Harry, m'boy! You're in luck the day. Got a nice delivery of black pudding in this morning.'

Guiding her to a table for two in a corner by the window—the glass of which looked as though it was held in by wishful thinking rather than anything else—Harry called back,

'Great, Mick. Could you bring two cups of tea while we look at the menu?'

'Done job.'

Gina sat down and tried not to stare at the assorted diners. There were lots of them, almost every table was full, and although some were what she'd term ordinary folk, there were others who were anything but that. One man was literally covered from head to foot in tattoos, his hooked nose being a hawk's body and with two wings sweeping across his cheeks, and there were a couple of Hell's Angels along with some gothic types in the far corner. More surprisingly still, a man in full evening-dress was sitting with a woman dripping with jewels, and both appeared to be half asleep.

Harry saw where she was looking. 'Mick gets a few Hooray Henrys from time to time,' he murmured. 'I gather this place is the latest rage with the hunt set after a night on the tiles.'

Mick was at their side before Gina could respond, his cheeky face split in a wide grin as he placed two huge, steaming mugs of tea on the table, all the time looking at her. 'Aren't you going to introduce us, Harry?'

'Mick, Gina. Gina, Mick.'

Mick nodded. 'Pleased to meet you, Gina.'

She smiled. There was something immensely likeable about this funny little man. 'Likewise, Mick.'

'Harry going to treat you to one of my big breakfast bonanzas, then?' Mick asked cheerfully. 'Eggs, bacon, sausages, hash browns, baked beans, tomatoes, black pudding and mushrooms, along with a couple of rounds of toast?' He paused, cocking his head as he surveyed her through bright black eyes.

Gina felt as though it was some sort of test. 'Sounds great.'

'I like her.' Mick turned to Harry approvingly. 'And I'm

pleased you've found yourself a good woman at last.' Focusing on Gina again, he added, 'I've been on at him ever since he first set foot over the threshold to find himself a nice lassie.'

She blinked, but the twinkle in Mick's beady eyes was disarming. 'How do you know I'm a nice lassie?' she returned, grinning. 'Perhaps Harry prefers the other sort.'

Mick shook his head. 'No, he's not as daft as he looks. He knows which side his bread's buttered, all right.'

'When you two have quite finished...' Harry's voice was dry in the extreme.

'Two bonanzas coming up.' Mick trotted off happily.

Gina took a sip of her tea and then looked up to see Harry watching her thoughtfully, his dark eyes serious. 'What?' she said nervously.

'Is there anyone or anything you can't handle?' he murmured with warm approval.

Feeling as though she'd just been given a million dollars, Gina wondered what his reaction would be if she admitted the answer to his question was sitting opposite her. 'Of course not,' she said lightly. 'I'm a modern woman, didn't you know? We can handle any problem that comes our way, and do it while juggling a hundred and one other things, incidentally. Unlike the male of the species.'

She had decided a minute ago that the only way she would be able to deal with Harry, Mick and this whole surreal morning was to keep things on a humorous level from now on.

He smiled. Her heart melted.

'The old one about men can only do one thing at a time?' he asked lazily. 'Whereas women are miracle workers.'

'Absolutely.' She couldn't help her heartbeat speeding up just a fraction, or the way her breath caught in her throat. He looked so altogether *sexy* sitting there; the way his smile mellowed the hard, handsome lines of his face was silver-screen material.

And then, because she couldn't resist asking, although she knew she shouldn't, she said, 'What did Mick mean about you finding yourself a woman at last? You've had girlfriends since you've been back in England.'

He shrugged. 'Not ones I'd choose to have breakfast with.' He paused, then added, 'And none I'd take home either.'

Warning herself none of that meant a thing, she murmured, 'The entanglement thing?'

'Self-protection would be a better description.'

He was staring at her, his emotions for once openly displayed in his gaze. Gina swallowed, jerking her eyes away as she warned herself she couldn't trust her sight where Harry was concerned—or the rest of her senses, come to that. She wanted him too much. It was too easy to project what she *wanted* to imagine she was seeing and hearing. And back there in the car he'd made no mention of commitment when he'd propositioned her, no hint that he saw her differently from all the others.

Nevertheless, her eyes on the mug of tea, she said quietly, 'You took *me* to your home.'

'Yes, I did.'

The tiny voice deep inside prompted her to carry on, 'Because we're friends?'

'If you're asking *only* friends, then I think we both know that was never true. I appreciate your friendship, Gina, I have all along, but on my part there was something more and I can't help that. I've wanted you from the first moment I saw you.'

'Physically.' She looked at him squarely, praying her face was as expressionless as she needed it to be.

'There was an immediate physical attraction, yes. I'm a man, I can't help it. Then…' He paused. 'I got to know *you.*'

Gina's movements were slow and deliberate as she picked up her mug and took several sips of the scalding-hot tea. If ever she needed the boost of caffeine it was now. Warning herself to remain outwardly calm, she said, 'I'm confused, Harry. Are you saying the self-protection thing is wearing thin? And, if so, why now?'

Did he know her whole body had stilled as she waited for his answer? she thought in the next heartbeat.

'Because it's time?' he suggested softly.

It was an answer, and yet not an answer. Was he saying in the future he intended to let his girlfriends have more access into his life? Certainly his emotions had been in cold storage for over a decade, by his own admission. Dredging up a smile, she lifted her eyes to his. 'So you started off with four little canines but hope to progress to bigger things?' she asked lightly. 'Something along those lines?'

He smiled back, but only with his mouth. 'I wouldn't put it quite like that.' He leant forward in his chair, his expression suddenly intense. 'The thing is, Gina—'

'Two bonanzas as ordered, and the toast's coming.' Neither of them had noticed Mick's approach, and Gina could have kicked the jovial little man. Instead she forced herself to smile politely as he placed one loaded plate in front of her and the other in front of Harry. How was she going to eat a morsel with her stomach doing cartwheels and her heart threatening palpitations?

As soon as Mick had scurried off, she said, 'You were saying?'

He stared at her for a moment. 'It doesn't matter. It would

be a case of rushing in where angels fear to tread, the way things are.'

She opened her mouth to ask him what he meant just as Mick said, 'Here's the toast. More tea for anyone?'

Go away. 'I'm fine,' she said brightly as Harry shook his head.

Mick obviously wasn't the most sensitive of souls, because the next moment he hooked himself a chair from another table and sat down beside Harry. 'That business plan you advised me to look into?' he said in a low voice. 'I've decided to do it.'

Harry inclined his head. 'Good.'

'I mean, like you said, I'm not necessarily committing to anything, am I? And the way profits are piling up, it's a good time. How do I set the ball rolling?'

Gina sighed inwardly. End of intimate discussion. Now she had to make some attempt at eating this enormous breakfast when all she wanted to do was to burst into tears. She revised her earlier opinion and decided she didn't like Mick at all.

CHAPTER ELEVEN

IT WAS just after half-past ten when they pulled up outside the house in which Gina's flat was situated later that morning.

When Mick had left their table after a few minutes of unashamedly picking Harry's brains, the resulting conversation had been inconsequential and light. Harry had made sure of that, acknowledging Mick's interruption had been timely.

What had he been doing, going in there with all the finesse of a charging bull-elephant? he asked himself now as he glanced at Gina's withdrawn face. It was the one thing he'd promised himself he wouldn't do when he'd suggested breakfast earlier. That had been a bad idea, too. Hell, this whole thing was a bad idea. He should have cut his losses when he'd found out about this other guy. Masochism had never been his scene.

And kissing her. He groaned mentally. Biggest mistake of all. He'd been as hard as a rock ever since. A hot arrow of humiliation zinged through him as the full weight of his vulnerability where Gina was concerned hit home. She could tie him up in knots with one glance from those blue eyes, and that wasn't good. Time to back-pedal.

Cutting the engine, he stretched his legs as far as he could in the close confines of the car, saying easily, 'I'm full. Mick's breakfasts always make me feel I need a visit to the gym in atonement, all that fat and so on. So, handover at eleven, you said?'

She nodded, a wisp of hair that had escaped the ponytail on top of her head skimming her cheek.

He wondered how such a simple thing could cause a further problem with a certain part of his anatomy. Although it wasn't simple. *She* wasn't simple. He'd thought she was accessible, soft and tender—and she was, in a way. But the defencelessness he'd sensed had a thick steel armour over it where the male of the species was concerned, thanks to this jerk who had let her down so badly. Knowing her as he'd imagined he did, seeing her every week-day and working with her so closely, hadn't prepared him for the guarded wariness that clothed her out of the office.

But perhaps she'd always been this way. He'd been so tied up with how *he'd* been feeling, would he have noticed? He had taken her absolutely for granted, and it was galling to admit he didn't know how to handle this new Gina.

'Need any help with anything?' He heard himself make the offer with a sense of shock. He had intended a swift goodbye and then an even swifter exit, the way things had gone.

She shook her head. 'No, I'm fine.'

'I don't think you're fine, Gina.' In spite of himself he leant forward and touched her mouth in the gentlest of kisses, drawing on every scrap of his considerable willpower to draw away in the next instant. 'And I'm sorry things have turned out this way.'

'This way?'

For a moment he was startled by the look on her face. 'You having to leave because of this guy.' He wasn't going to ask for her address again. If she offered it, he would know he had a chance.

She got out of the car. He joined her, his smile the best bit of acting he'd done for a long while as he said, 'Guess this is goodbye, then? Shame; Daisy and crew would have loved to have seen more of you.

'They've got you,' she whispered, without raising her eyes.

She looked very small and unprotected, and his guts were in spasm with the effort it was taking not to gather her into his arms. He wondered how someone so small and cuddly looking could be so formidable. And how he could have been so blind and stupid for so long.

Taking a woman to bed had become a pleasant pastime since Anna, but nothing more. Physically satisfying—even, on occasion, mentally stimulating too—but that was all. But from the day he'd met Gina an unsettled feeling had begun to grow, slowly and insidiously at first. The more he'd tried to ignore it, the more it had nagged at him, but still he'd been too damn stubborn to take notice. He'd wasted months mess-ing about, months when he could have been persuading her this creep she was mixed up with was history. But he'd been scared. Scared of what he felt, scared of being out of control, scared of so many things he couldn't even put a name to some of them.

So was he going to let her walk out of his life because he was too proud to persist where he obviously wasn't wanted? Or was he going to make her want him?

'Yes, Daisy and crew have got me,' he agreed softly, keeping his voice easy and steady. 'But I'm an old-fashioned kind of guy at heart. You know: the man does the discipline and "this is for your own good" routine, and the woman undoes it all and spoils the kids rotten.'

She raised her face, a small smile on her lips, although he

could swear they were trembling. 'All the women I know would call you a male-chauvinist pig for that remark.'

'I never said I was perfect.' He shrugged, smiling. 'But then, you know that.'

'Yes, I know that.'

'And, because I'm a selfish so-and-so, I really don't want to lose touch with the one woman in my life I can *talk* to. I mean that, Gina.' He reached out and took her chin in his hand, enjoying the soft feel of her skin. He noticed a peculiar look in her eyes, and wondered for a moment if she found his touch repellent. But when her mouth had been under his he knew she'd responded to him, he told himself in the next instant. 'I know you want to cut ties with your old life, but face facts. Your parents are here, your sisters, your friends. It won't be as easy as that. They'll all be dropping in to see you now and again, and you'll be visiting them. I insist on being added to the list, OK?'

She took a step backwards and he dropped his hand. 'I've told you, I don't think that's a good idea, Harry.'

'And I've told you I disagree.' He held up his hands. 'OK, so I was a bit out of order suggesting what I did earlier, but there's nothing to stop us remaining friends.'

Her sigh was really more of a shudder. She hooked a strand of silken red hair behind her ear and gave what sounded like a nervous laugh. 'Same old Harry,' she said, shaking her head. 'You're just not very good at taking no for an answer, are you?'

'Terrible,' he agreed. 'Fault since childhood.'

She met his gaze then. He tried to keep his features open and friendly, and nothing more. 'Did it ever occur to you I can be equally as determined?' she asked quietly.

'Oh yes.' He looked down into those beautiful blue eyes that were strangely veiled this morning. An increase in pressure from somewhere inside his chest made it difficult for him to breathe for a long moment. He was aware of birds chirruping in the trees lining the road, of a dog barking somewhere in the distance and the sound of children playing in a garden close by, but the world was narrowed down to two deep, violet orbs. 'But I think you're a pretty sensible woman at heart,' he said as lightly as he could. 'The odd meal together, a visit to the theatre or the cinema, you joining me in taking the dogs for a walk when you're in these parts—what's wrong with that? All gain, no pain.'

The parody of a smile twisted her features. 'A pretty sensible woman,' she echoed, but he heard the tremor in her voice. 'Sensible women don't let themselves be hurt by egotistical, self-centred men, do they?'

Him again. He'd like five minutes in a soundproof room with this guy. By the time he'd finished with him, even his own mother wouldn't have recognised him. Taking a deep pull of air, he shrugged. 'Not habitually, which only bears out what I'm saying. You tried, it didn't work, he didn't appreciate what he'd got, you're leaving. That sounds sensible to me.'

She was quiet for a long moment. In the distance the dog had stopped barking and the children must have been called indoors. Even the birds had stopped their frenzied twittering. Suddenly it was very silent.

He saw her take a long swallow before she said, 'Harry, I can see I have to tell you something.'

His eyes narrowed. Whatever she was going to say, he wasn't going to like it; her body language told him so. There was nothing short of an expression of doom on her face. He shoved his hands into the pockets of his jeans, because it was either that or take her in his arms and force her to acknowledge the physical attraction between them. OK, so it wasn't love like she felt for this bozo, but it was a start. Plenty of people had built something on less. 'Go ahead,' he said flatly. 'I'm all ears.'

'What I told you about my going to London is true...' she began jerkily, only to pause and glance over his shoulder a second before Harry registered someone calling her name. Raising her hand in response, Gina said quickly, 'It's my estate agent with the new owners. I have to go.'

'Wait.' He caught her arm. 'Not yet. What were you going to say?'

'It doesn't matter.' Her withdrawal had been quick and complete.

He stared at her in frustration. However unpalatable it was, he knew it had been important. 'The hell it doesn't,' he said softly. 'Tell me, whatever it is. The estate agent can wait.'

It appeared he couldn't. The next moment the man was at their side, the young couple who were with him standing a few yards away. 'We said eleven o'clock, Gina,' the man said with a toothy—and, to Harry, insincere—smile. 'I trust there's not a problem?'

Harry glanced at his watch pointedly. 'You've ten minutes to go,' he said coolly, his eyes icy. 'And there's no problem, other than that you happen to be interrupting an important conversation.

The man blinked. 'Well, really!'

'You go in, Robert.' Gina was as red as her hair, something which made him even more angry with the estate agent— irrationally, Harry acknowledged. 'I'll be with you in a moment.' The instant the three had disappeared, she rounded on him. 'I can't believe you could be so rude.'

'Having known me for twelve months, I doubt that.'

'This is not funny, Harry.'

'Who's laughing?' He found himself glaring at her, which was the last thing he wanted to do. Warning himself to calm down, he said more reasonably, 'The guy was downright ignorant, Gina, and you know it. His whole attitude was—' He stopped abruptly. 'Hell, what are we wasting time talking about him for? What were you going to say?'

She shook her head helplessly. 'You're unbelievable.' It wasn't laudatory. 'And it would take too long now. Another time.'

Harry had taken the last seconds to put his voice into neutral. 'Fine. I'll wait till you're finished with the suit.'

'No, not now. I—' She shook her head again. 'I'll phone you, all right?'

'Is that in the same context as giving me your address? Because if so I get the impression I'll wait a long time,' he ground out with grim honesty.

She searched his face for a long moment. He tried to keep his features expressionless. Then she said slowly, 'I don't want to have this conversation any more. I've got a long and tiring day in front of me, and you're not helping. Please go.' She turned her head away as though she couldn't bear to look at him.

'Fine.' The rage that swept over him was stronger than anything he'd felt before, even in the worst times with Anna. 'Goodbye, Gina.'

'Goodbye.'

Her voice had changed, the cold note had gone to be replaced with a huskiness. A pain he had not thought possible knifed through his chest and took the capacity for further speech away. He couldn't reach her, he realised painfully.

And he couldn't tolerate any more of this without saying something he'd regret in hindsight.

He would have turned and walked away at that instant, if she hadn't raised her eyes and looked at him. The emptiness and stark desolation were too much. Nothing on earth could have stopped what happened next.

At first she resisted being in his arms, but then as his mouth continued its sensual assault she started to shake; he could feel it. He kissed her as he had wanted to do all morning since that first embrace in the car, his hands moving up and down her back as he moulded her into the hard length of him. The innate softness of her, the tantalising warmth of her perfume on silky skin, her lips open beneath his, all added to the fire that had taken him over, and he made no effort to pull back. Helplessly he devoured her mouth; desire was a flame inside him spreading rapidly. The need was too hot to resist.

She was sweet, potent. The taste, the smell of her, spun in his head and he knew she was with him; the tiny, uncontrolled moans against his mouth told him so. Whatever this other man meant to her, he—Harry Breedon—could make her tremble and sigh. And if sexual desire was all there was at first, he would use it as ruthlessly as he had to.

Using all his considerable experience, he skilfully demanded her submission, his lips moving to her long neck as she quivered in his hold. Her head was back, her eyes closed, her throat laid bare and vulnerable, and he heard himself groan with pleasure as he ran his lips over the honey, freckled skin.

'Gina, Gina.' He breathed her name against the scented flesh, revelling in her closeness. The feel of her firm breasts against the wall of his chest was a compelling aphrodisiac, and for a second he marvelled that she could move him so fiercely when they were both still fully clothed. She must be aware of the powerful attraction their bodies held for each other, the way every nerve and sinew was honed into the other's desire. The pulse in her throat was racing madly, proving she was as aroused as he was.

And then the quiet, sleepy nature of the empty street was shattered as the roar of a motorbike broke the silence. Although he registered the sound at the same moment as she broke the kiss and jerked away, he tried to hold on to her.

'No, Harry.' She pushed against him. 'Please, let me go.'

'Gina—'

'I mean it, I don't want this. *No!*'

When she pushed again he let her go free, his voice husky as he said, 'You see? You see how it could be between us? You can't deny there's something special, Gina. I want you, and I know you want me. Your body tells me so.'

She stared at him, her big blue eyes wide with what he put down to shock at what had transpired between them. The motorbike flashed past them, going much too fast for a lazy Saturday morning. 'There has to be more than sexual satisfaction for me, Harry. It wouldn't be enough, however well our bodies fitted together.'

He raked back his hair, frustration and irritation at her stubbornness vying with the need to make her *see*. 'Was it as good for you with this other guy?' he ground out. 'Could he turn you on with one kiss?'

She continued to look at him, her face white under the sprinkling of freckles. Slowly the sound of the bike receded and the scented quiet of the morning took over again. 'Yes,' she said at last.

'Was it better, just because you think you love him? Can you truthfully tell me that?'

Again she stared at him for long moments, not moving a muscle. He wished he knew what was going on behind the blue gaze. He was barely breathing as he waited for her answer, his chest tight.

'I don't think I love him,' she said so softly he could barely hear her. 'I know I do. I always will. And, however good sex might be with someone else, it couldn't begin to compare with the briefest of kisses from him. I can't change that, Harry. I don't want to change it. And I don't want any other man touching me or kissing me. Only him. That's the way I'm made.'

He felt sick inside, his insides twisting at the ring of truth in her voice. He had pushed it, he told himself, and this was his answer. He only had himself to blame.

Years of training made his face a blank mask. 'I see.' He nodded, a crisp movement, while his eyes remained locked on hers. 'Then I'm sorry for you, because he won't change. Men like him never do.'

'I know that.' There was a wealth of sadness in her smile. 'Goodbye, Harry. I hope you find what you're looking for some day.'

I did. I have. 'Goodbye, Gina.' He couldn't return the smile. 'Good luck.'

Without another word she turned from him and walked towards the house. He stood staring after her, wondering if she would look round and wave when she had opened the door. She didn't. The door closed behind her, and all was still.

He continued to stand where he was for a full minute, feeling as if his feet had been glued to the floor. But it wasn't his feet that were the problem, he told himself grimly once he was seated in his car. It was his heart. And his brain. Somehow he had to get his head round the fact that he was not going to see her again, because if ever a woman had meant what she said, Gina had.

His chest rose and fell as he took in deep breaths, trying to clear his scrambled thoughts and shake off the bitter regret that he had pushed things to their ultimate conclusion. It would have happened anyway, he consoled himself bleakly. Tomorrow, the next day, the next week or month, whenever he had seen her again. *If* he had seen her again. Which he doubted. She had been determined to keep her whereabouts hidden all along, he just hadn't accepted what was under his nose.

So, what now? He started the car, drawing away from the kerb after checking his mirrors and warning himself to concentrate. He couldn't go back to the way he was before he'd met her, more especially before he had acknowledged just what she meant to him. And the peripatetic life held no appeal now. He had promised his father he'd build the business into a good, marketable position in order for it to be sold before he pulled out, calculating that would mean a period of two, three years at the most. And then he'd imagined he'd take off again for pastures new.

Damn it! He drove his fist against the steering wheel, swearing long and loud. It didn't help. Why did she have to be a one-man woman, anyway? He'd spent the last decade around women who had cultivated a cool, philosophical attitude to life and love, women who were rational and logical, who cut their losses when a relationship came to an end and moved on serenely to the next man. Why couldn't Gina be like one of them?

Because then she wouldn't be Gina, and he wouldn't have fallen in love with her. Much good that it had done him.

His heart felt as though it was being squeezed by a giant hand, and he made a deep impatient sound in his throat. He didn't want to feel like this, damn it. He didn't want to be drowning helplessly in his own emotions. This was everything he had fought to avoid since his marriage. Perhaps it was best she was in love with someone else if this was what she did to him. She'd have had him running round in circles.

It was empty comfort. Which matched the future pretty well, he thought bleakly. How he was going to get through the rest of his life, he didn't know.

CHAPTER TWELVE

'GINA, I hate to be so boring as to state the obvious, but it's Friday night and you're in the big city. Moreover, this is the umpteenth time you've refused to come out with the girls. What do I have to do to get you to party?'

Gina smiled at the tall, skinny girl sitting cross-legged on her bed. Candy was an attractive, languid brunette whose somewhat vague, dreamy exterior hid the fact that she was in fact an extremely intelligent and successful career-woman with a responsible position in a merchant bank. She was also genuinely nice, something Gina had learned in the first twenty-four hours of being in London, when she had broken down so completely she hadn't been able to hide she was a total emotional mess.

From keeping her love for Harry hidden from everyone at home, even her mother, she had found herself telling Candy everything that first weekend, getting through a couple of boxes of tissues in the process. And Candy had responded magnificently, offering unlimited concern and sympathy, and calling Harry every name under the sun. Since then she had taken it as her mission in life to initiate Gina into the party scene, even though Gina had resisted to date.

'Look.' Candy leant forward, her big brown eyes earnest. 'You've been in London over two months, and it's a gorgeous June evening, much too nice to be stuck indoors. And don't say you're going to go on one of your endless walks, because that's not the sort of outdoors I mean.'

Gina's smile widened. 'You mean the sort of stuffy-night-club outdoors, I take it?'

Candy rolled her eyes. 'A nightclub full of good-looking guys who are positively *aching* for you to make an entrance.'

'Yeah, right.' She couldn't help laughing. 'I don't think so, somehow, Candy.'

'You'll never know if you don't try it. And there's safety in numbers. Kath and Linda and Nikki are coming, and Lucy and Samantha. Even if one or two of us get lucky, there'll be someone to get a cab home with. It's not *good* for you to stay in moping all the time.'

'I don't, and you know it.' Gina decided a little firmness was in order. 'But the club scene doesn't do it for me.'

'How do you know, if you don't try it?' Candy wailed.

'I don't *want* to meet anyone at the moment.'

'So just come out and have a good time with the girls,' Candy said promptly. 'We're going to eat first, and then go on to Blades or the Edition. You've met everyone, you like them and they like you. Just let your hair down for once. Have a dance and act silly. Flirt. Tease. You know.'

Actually she didn't, but Candy's grin was infectious. 'You aren't going to be satisfied until you see me bleary-eyed and hung over like you on a Saturday morning, are you?' she said resignedly.

'Is that a yes?' Candy whooped her delight. 'Great. We can do the girly thing of deciding what to wear in a minute. I've missed that since Jennie swapped the good life for boring old matrimony.' Jennie, Candy's previous flatmate of some years standing, had decided to opt and get married, much to Candy's disgust. Having been brought up by her mother after her father had run out on his wife and two children when Candy was five, Gina's flatmate was determined never to walk down the aisle.

It was only when Gina began to try on some of the more dressy items in her wardrobe that she realised just how much weight she'd lost in the last few weeks. She'd noticed her work skirts were looser, of course, and buttons she'd struggled with in the past were no longer a problem, but she liked to feel comfortable at work, and the easy fit had been agreeable. It wasn't as though she had dieted or anything, the pounds had simply melted away due to hectic busy days and restless evenings spent walking in the surrounding district until she was tired enough to drop into bed and go straight to sleep.

She had always longed to be slimmer, but now it had actually happened she found she wasn't sure if she liked her new shape or not. Or perhaps it was the small lines of misery which seemed to have taken residence between her brows, and the faint, bruised-looking shadows beneath her eyes she didn't like. Whatever, she discovered her favourite couple of dresses didn't look right at all.

She saw Candy look at her as she stood in front of the mirror in her room. The sleeveless sheer twisted-tulle dress with an attached shift beneath was perfectly suited to an evening such as this, but suddenly it hung on her like a sack. With a quick 'Hang on a sec,' Candy disappeared, returning a moment later with a wide and frighteningly expensive soft leather belt she had bought the weekend before.

'Here.' Candy thrust the belt at her. 'I think this will look fabulous with that dress. I must have been thinking of you when I bought it.'

'You haven't even worn it yet.'

Gina tried to give it back but Candy was having none of it, and when she tried it on she had to admit the cream-coloured belt against the seductive, taupe dress gave her a waist that appeared about eighteen inches wide, emphasising her hourglass shape in a way that made Candy groan with envy.

'What I'd give for a bust like yours, but after seeing a few horror stories on the TV and in magazines I know I'm not brave enough to go under the knife for it.' Candy grimaced as she adjusted her sparkly top over her 32A cups with a deep sigh. 'I don't care what men say about some of them being a leg man, they all love a girl with plenty up top.'

'Some not enough, though.'

Their eyes met in the mirror, and immediately Candy pulled a face. 'No, none of that, I forbid it. You're not thinking of him tonight, Gina. This evening is strictly a Harry-free zone, OK?'

'OK.' Gina wondered—and not for the first time—how she would have got through the last nine weeks but for her flatmate. The utter desolation she had felt over Harry, the considerable pressure of taking on a new job along with a complete change of environment, had all been difficult to a greater or lesser degree, but Candy had been there for her one hundred and ten per cent.

Comforter, clown, advisor—whatever Gina's need had been, Candy had delivered. Her flatmate was one of those wonderful, irrepressible souls who would fit Gina's father's northern accolade of being 'salt of the earth', not that the highly independent and totally modern Candy would have particularly appreciated that, or any other label.

Gina grinned at her friend now as she said, 'You would actually like Harry if you met him, Candy. He's got the one thing you admire more than anything else: absolute honesty in his dealings with the opposite sex.'

Candy snorted. She had a huge repertoire of snorts, and they were infinitely more expressive than any words. 'He's one in a million, then,' she said darkly.

'Well, I'd agree with that of course, but then you know that. On a serious note—' She hesitated, then went on gently. 'All men aren't like your father, Candy.'

'I know that. There's always the exception to the rule but, believe me, Gina, most of them are motivated by what's in their trousers. And don't look at me like that, it's true. They're a different *species* to us, let alone a different sex. You have to play them at their own game to win. Take what you want when you want it and without getting involved heart-wise. It's the only way to remain your own person.'

'You sound more like Harry than Harry.'

'Perhaps we *would* get on, then.' Candy grinned. 'But you're far too nice for a man like that. Now, what shoes are you going to wear with that dress? Seriously sexy high-heels, I think. What have we got?'

Gina bent down and rifled through the bottom of her wardrobe before straightening and waving a pair of shoes in the same manner as a magician producing a rabbit out of a hat. 'These do?'

'Oh, wow, perfect.' Candy looked at the vertiginous, slinky court-shoes with their ruffled bow in the exact colour of the dress with respect. Gina didn't tell her that both the dress and shoes had been bought on a shopping trip with Bryony when her sister had insisted she buy something fabulous for a friend's wedding. Left to her own devices, she would probably have gone for something a little less eye-catching.

Now, taking the full credit for herself, she said smugly, 'Not bad for a little country yokel, eh?'

'Not bad at all.' Candy eyed her up and down. 'I tell you, girl, when you walk in that club tonight there's going to be more than one man straining at the leash. I'm going to make sure you're introduced to a new world of fun and frolicking, the like you've never dreamt of, or my name isn't Candy Robinson.'

Gina's smile dimmed. She didn't want a world of fun and frolicking unless it included Harry. Fun and frolicking with him would be an entirely different kettle of fish, though.

Proving 'mind reader' could be added to her CV, Candy waved a reproving finger. 'Stop it this minute. I told you, Harry-free zone tonight. I'm going to pour us both an enormous glass of wine while we do our hair in some outrageous style. Feathers I think for tonight, and I've got a sparkly spray in a wonderful shade of pink that'll wash out tomorrow morning.'

Gina stared at her in horror. 'Pink? With my hair? I don't think so, Candy.'

'OK, perhaps not the spray for you, then, but a spiky top-knot with a couple of my feathers would look funky.'

Gina nodded resignedly. 'Whatever you think.'

'Good girl. You know it makes sense.'

Despite her qualms, Gina had to admit that by the time they were ready to leave she looked good, thanks to Candy. She didn't look like herself, she didn't *feel* like herself, but that— Candy insisted firmly—was part of the fun. Certainly, in her bubblegum-pink dress and with streaks of vivid pink in her hair Candy was as different from the neat businesswoman of daylight hours as the man in the moon.

'I just love dressing up,' Candy said happily, finishing the last of her wine and smacking her lips. 'I don't think I've ever grown up, to be honest, which is why I'm the worst person in the world to have kids.'

'Not necessarily,' Gina said rationally. 'Being childlike in certain respects could mean you connect better with children, if anything.'

This time the snort expressed scorn. 'I don't like kids,' Candy stated firmly. 'Too demanding, too time-consuming, too messy. You can't do what you want when the mood takes you if you've got a kid to consider, let alone a husband. And carrying a baby for nine months…gross. My mum was really pretty in the photos she's got before she had us, but now she looks ten years older than what she is.'

'It doesn't have to be that way.'

Candy looked at her as she reached for her light cotton waist-length cardigan. 'You'd really choose to give up your freedom for eighteen, twenty-odd years to bring up some man's children?'

'Not *some man's*, no.'

'Oh, no, he's back, isn't he?'

Gina flushed. 'You asked, so I told you, and to be honest I can't think of anything more wonderful than being with him and having his babies. Sorry, but that's me.'

'So why didn't you take what he offered and then accidentally-on-purpose fall pregnant or something? That would have kept you in his life, if nothing else.'

'I couldn't have done that.' Gina was appalled.

Candy surveyed her for a long moment. 'No, I don't suppose you could,' she said softly. 'And you know what? He's a fool, this Harry of yours.'

This was getting too heavy before a night on the tiles. Gina forced a smile. 'Now, there I *would* agree with you,' she said lightly. She put her half-full glass of wine on the table as she spoke. When Candy had spoken about large glasses she'd meant large glasses—glass buckets would be a better description. If she finished this, she would be in no fit state to walk, let alone go to the nightclub. She was already feeling light-headed. 'Come on, then,' she said, linking her arm through Candy's. 'Let's go and meet the others. I'm starving.'

They clattered down the stairs from their second-floor flat in the tall Victorian terrace, giggling and talking. Candy opened the door into the street, stepping backwards in the next moment right on Gina's toe. Candy's gasp of surprise and Gina's yelp of pain intermingled, before a deep male voice said, 'Sorry. I didn't mean to make you jump. I was just about to ring the bell.'

Gina's lips formed his name, but her locked throat uttered no sound. Candy glanced at her and then back to the tall, dark man standing on the step. Her tone dry, she said coolly, 'I take it you're Harry Breedon?'

Harry's eyes had been intent on Gina. Now there was a flash of surprise apparent as he glanced at Candy for a moment. 'Yes. How did you know?'

'Are you kidding?'

His brow wrinkled, but, his gaze returning to Gina, he said softly, 'How are you?'

'She's fine.' Candy was clearly determined to imitate a pit bull terrier. 'Next question.'

Gina knew she had to say something, had to stop the potential disaster that could occur with Candy in this mood, but the power of speech was beyond her. In fact if it hadn't been for the wall she was leaning against she'd have been on the floor at his feet, her legs having turned to jelly.

She was terrified Candy might say something indiscreet, especially in view of the amount of wine her flatmate had consumed on an empty stomach, and she was bitterly regretting having confided in the other girl. She had just never considered Candy and Harry would ever meet.

Harry's gaze had switched back to Candy, and now there was pure steel in the smoky-grey eyes, his facial muscles having tightened ominously. 'Forgive me,' he said with silky menace, 'But I don't think we've met?'

Physical and mental intimidation had no effect on Candy. She stared back at him as though he was something that had just crawled out from under a stone.

From somewhere Gina found the strength to croak, 'Please, Candy, leave it,' before turning to Harry and saying, 'What are you doing here?'

His eyes had narrowed, but he drew in a deep pull of air before he said, 'I was passing, and I thought I'd drop in and see how you are.'

Candy's flat chest swelled to glamour-model proportions. 'Is that "see how you are" meaning a quickie, or "see how you are" meaning I'm sorry I've screwed you up so badly?' she asked scathingly.

Gina closed her eyes. The silence was profound. Then one exploding *'What?'* reverberated. When she opened her eyes, Harry's face was blazing with fury. 'I'm not sure where you're coming from, lady,' he ground out at Candy, 'But you're way off-beam.'

Candy's hands were on her hips, her body bent slightly forwards, but before she could say anything else Gina intervened. 'That's right, she's got it all wrong,' she said desperately. 'But we have to go. We're late already—'

'No way.' To Gina's horror he literally barred the way. 'Not till I find out what the hell is going on. *You*—' The razor-sharp gaze cut into Candy's indignant face. 'I don't know what you're thinking here, but Gina and I are friends, OK? From back home.'

Candy turned to Gina. Taking in the look on her face, she appeared to suddenly deflate. 'I'm sorry, I didn't mean to—' She stopped abruptly. 'But you ought to say something, you know that at heart. You can't move on till you do, the way you're made.'

'Candy, *please*,' Gina pleaded in anguish.

'Excuse me, but am I missing something here?' Harry said icily. And then, as both women stood, surveying him dumbly, he glanced from one to the other. 'Right, at the risk of making you even later, we're all having a nice little chat. In the street, in a taxi, wherever, but I'm not budging till I get an answer. Along with an apology,' he added grimly, shooting a glance at Candy.

'An *apology*?' Candy was back in fighting mode. 'Over my dead body.'

'Not an unappealing thought,' Harry returned tightly.

'Look, you rat—'

'Stop it.' There was a note in Gina's voice that brought a cessation in hostilities. With two pairs of eyes on her face, she said flatly, 'We'll talk upstairs in the flat, Harry. You go, Candy. Tell the others I'm not coming.'

'I'm not leaving you alone with him.'

'For crying out loud!' Harry looked ready to explode. 'What the hell do you think I'm going to do to her?'

'I'm not going.' Ignoring Harry, Candy pursed her lips at Gina. 'Not till I know you're going to be all right.'

'I'll be fine.'

'I'm still not going.'

She couldn't cope with the pair of them standing there with mulish frowns. Gina fought down the sudden flood of pure irritation filling her chest as she reflected *she* was the one who had every right to be awkward here. *She* was the one who had been telling herself for weeks that people didn't waste away from unrequited love these days, and that she had to keep going, that she wasn't going to allow anyone to ruin her life. *She* had walked herself into the ground every evening so she could sleep at night. *She* was the one who had battled against the devastating truth that she would never marry, never have children, a truth that had threatened to crush her more times than she could remember.

Her voice sharp, she said crisply, 'We'd better go upstairs, then, the three of us.' And she turned before either of them could react. Marching ahead, she wished she'd worn shoes other than ones which required her to sway so provocatively just to balance. She had seen the look in Harry's eyes when he had first taken in her appearance. It had been shock, she knew it. Did he think she had dressed like this purely to get a man tonight? That two months in the city had turned her into a man-eater?

It doesn't matter what he thinks. This thought was so ludicrous she dismissed it in the next moment. It mattered. It mattered so much she felt faint.

Gina opened the flat's front door with fingers that trembled, and walked through to the small sitting-room. She turned to face him. Candy had sidled in and already sat down, but Harry was still standing in the doorway.

'Can I get you a drink?' she asked with rigid self-control,

knowing in the next few minutes she was about to humiliate herself utterly. Because Candy had been right, down there in the hall—she *did* have to tell Harry how she felt about him, if only so he would leave her alone. And he would, oh, he would. He would run a mile once he knew she cared, *really* cared, about him.

Was that why she had not said anything before? Because a tiny part of her—a really weird, tiny part probably—hadn't been able to face the final, no-hope goodbye? Candy had spoken about her moving on, but she didn't *want* to move on into a world in which Harry played no part—even on the distant perimeter. But neither could a situation like the one tonight happen again, she did see that.

'I don't want a drink, Gina,' Harry said with cold control. 'And explanation would be good, though. Since when did my name become synonymous with the Marquis de Sade?'

She took a deep breath. Truth time. And maybe it was better to tell him looking like this—as someone else. Perhaps he would think that, however she felt about him, she was determined to build a full and satisfying life for herself.

'This is not Candy's fault,' she said shakily. 'She is only reacting to what I've told her.'

A muscle in his cheek twitched and the sensual mouth tightened. 'Which is?'

She hesitated. *Coward*, she screamed inside. *Say it. Tell him.*

Harry took a step into the room and then stopped. His lips were white with anger, she noticed with the part of her brain that was still registering facts. 'Hell, woman,' he ground out. 'What do you want from me? I backed off when you made it clear how you felt, I rolled over and played dead. So I turn up tonight, is that a crime?'

'No.' It wasn't. Not really. She couldn't blame him for following through and contacting her, after the way she had responded sexually to him that last morning. And, seeing her tonight, he'd think she was game for anything! 'No, it's not a crime.'

'So what did I do that was so bad as to get the sort of reaction your friend gave me tonight, eh? Now, if it had been that cretin who messed up your head so badly—'

He stopped. Whether it was the movement of Candy behind him, or the look on her face, Gina wasn't sure, but suddenly she saw incredulity in the hard, handsome face. Wishing the floor would open and swallow her, she forced herself to stand straight. There would be time afterwards, all the time in the world, to crumple. For now it was desperately important she faced him with her head held high. Because he knew.

'I didn't want you to know,' she said dully. 'It was better you didn't know, for both of us.'

She could see the highly intelligent brain trying to assimilate the knowledge that had been thrust at it. His eyes were blank, expressionless, as he struggled to come to terms with the fact he was the man who had driven her away.

'I don't believe it.' He moved his head in a rapid movement, signifying a silent apology for his disbelief. 'Why—why didn't you tell me? You're saying I—' He stopped, clearly still unable to believe what he knew she was saying.

Gina knew what it was to die a hundred times before she could bring herself to answer. 'You're the man I love, Harry. There's no one else, there never has been. I guess I'm what is quaintly called a one-man woman. That means for me it's all or nothing.'

He stared at her for an endless moment. And then she watched, unbelieving, as the most beautiful smile lit up his face. He covered the distance between them in a heartbeat, neither of them hearing Candy's 'Whoa,' of protest.

'Why didn't you tell me?' He pulled her into his arms with enough force to make her feathered top-knot bob precariously. 'Why put us both through torment?'

For a moment she thought she hadn't heard right, that the stress of his sudden appearance had addled her brain. Pulling back, she stared up into his face. 'You don't want anyone to—to love you,' she stammered helplessly.

'Not anyone, I want *you*.'

'No. You said you couldn't handle commitment, togetherness. You said that. And the way I feel…' She shook her head, trying to find the words to make him understand. 'It's for ever, Harry. And you said—'

'I said a damn sight too much, and all of it rubbish.'

She was in his arms, and he was looking at her in a way she had dreamt of in a thousand dreams, but still she didn't dare believe it. 'No,' she said again. 'You had girlfriends, you didn't look at me that way until you knew I was moving away, and there'd be no real commitment. But I can't be what you'd want me to be.'

'You *are* what I want you to be.' A soft sigh shuddered through his body and she felt the echo of it in hers. 'I've been going crazy without you, believe me. Stark staring crazy. The day you left I promised myself I wouldn't try to muscle in on you again, not when you'd told me there was no chance, that this guy would always be there. But it was no good. I couldn't eat, couldn't sleep.' He took a deep breath. 'I love you, Gina. And if I'm honest it frightens me to death. But I'm more frightened at the thought of living another day, another minute, without you.'

Neither of them knew Candy had left until they heard the click of the sitting-room door as she closed it behind her. 'Candy, she's gone,' Gina said vacantly, staring up into his face. 'I'm supposed to be going out with her tonight.'

'You're going nowhere unless it's with me.'

'But you didn't say you loved me.' Her voice was almost plaintive. 'You let me leave.'

'I thought you were madly in love with someone else, how could I tell you how I felt? It would only have been adding another reason for you to get away, or that's the way I saw it. But I tried to make you understand you were different—'

'No.' She didn't dare believe this because when he told her he had made a mistake, changed his mind, she would die. 'No, you aren't that sort of man.'

'What sort of man, my love?' he asked softly.

'My love.' Her breath caught at the words she'd never thought to hear from his lips, but still she couldn't let herself hope. 'The for ever kind.'

He gave a choked laugh and buried his face in the soft skin of her neck for a moment. 'I'm eternally for ever where you're concerned,' he said thickly, moulding her against him and holding her as though he would never let her go. 'Till death do us part and beyond. I realised that when you went away. If you don't want me I'm destined to live my life alone, apart from four rapidly growing small dogs, that is, who happen to be spending the weekend with my parents.'

Her arms wound around his neck tightly. If she didn't want him? What was he talking about? Surely he knew by now he was her world, the very air she breathed? 'How—how are the puppies?' she whispered dazedly.

'Missing you.' He lowered his head, crushing her soft lips

under his in a kiss that spoke of his profound hunger. He kissed her deeply, a long, lingering kiss, and when he finally raised his head she was sure her soul had merged with his. 'Marry me soon?' he murmured huskily. 'I mean *real* soon?'

Gina tried to ignore the effect his hand sliding up and down her back was having. It was difficult. Her breathing shallow, she said, 'Harry, are you sure?'

'That it has to be soon? Dead sure.'

'That…that you want to marry me. After what you've been through…' She took a deep breath, wondering if she should go on. 'I mean, after Anna and everything.'

Harry didn't even blink. 'I have never been more sure of anything in my life.' He covered her mouth in another hungry kiss that left her reeling. 'I want you for my wife. I want you as the mother of my children. But more than anything I want to make love to you every day for the rest of our lives.' He brushed a strand of hair from her forehead with infinite tenderness. 'All day, every day, and all night.'

She smiled, a wave of fierce desire washing over her body as she felt the hard ridge of his arousal against her softness. 'Just now and again, then?' she murmured teasingly.

'And again and again and again…'

Suddenly terrified that this was all a dream, she pressed into him, kissing him with an intensity that touched him to the core. Growling softly, he curved over her, the scent and feel of him encompassing her as he savoured the sweetness of her mouth. Her hands moved feverishly under the thin cotton shirt he was wearing, her fingers running over the shifting muscles of his back, then curling round to tangle themselves in the thick black hair of his chest, glorying in the warmth and strength of the hard male body. 'I didn't think I was ever going to see you again,' she half-sobbed against his mouth. 'I thought you wanted me for a brief affair, like all the others.'

'They didn't mean anything, Gina.' He raised his head, looking deep into her eyes. 'Not a thing. Does that disgust you?'

Nothing he had done or would ever do could disgust her. She shook her head.

'Looking back now, I'm not proud of the last ten years of my life, but I can't change them. What I can do is make sure you know every moment of every day from now on that you are the one and only woman for me. I knew twelve months ago, deep inside. I wouldn't admit it, even to myself, but there was something about you that tore at my heart even then.'

She thought of all the nights she'd cried herself to sleep, the heartache, loneliness and despair. Suddenly it didn't matter. It was worth it for this.

'I love you, Gina, with everything I am, every part of me,' he whispered, running his hands up and down her body as her fingers continued to trace the wide musculature of his chest. 'And we're going to do this right. I want our wedding night to be special, can you understand that?'

She nodded, loving him. It had all been so wrong with Anna. This time he wanted it to be different from the outset.

'But I'm only human.' As her hands moved over his body, his breath caught jaggedly. Catching her fingers in his, he breathed deeply before he said, 'I want you so badly it hurts. How much time do you need to get married?'

'No time at all.' She loosened one of her hands, reaching up and stroking the hard, male jaw. 'My sisters both had big weddings with bridesmaids and all the trimmings, and I hated every minute of them. I'd like to slip away somewhere, with just our parents in tow.' She smiled dreamily. 'A white dress for me, a light suit for you, with maybe a carnation in your buttonhole. No fuss and no frills, just the two of us saying our vows before God and man.'

He stared at her. 'You're an amazing woman.'

'It's taken you long enough to find that out.'

They each gave a small laugh before he picked her up and carried her over to the small sofa, sitting down with her on his lap and kissing her once more. She kissed him back with all her heart, and again it was Harry who applied the brake, his mouth leaving hers and trailing a row of nibbling kisses along her jawline.

Gina reached up and trailed her fingers through his crisp dark hair in a way she'd longed to do for more than twelve months. 'How did you find out my address?' she asked breathlessly, enchanted she could touch him like this.

'I lied to your mother.'

'What?' She stared at him, pulling back slightly to look into his face and see if he was serious.

'I phoned her in the capacity of your ex-boss and said there were a couple of things the account department needed to forward to you for your new employers. Fortunately, she didn't ask what they were.' He paused. 'Do I take it you hadn't told her how you felt about me? Because she seemed very friendly. I'd have thought if she knew I'd driven her daughter away she might have been a little less polite.'

'I didn't tell anyone, not till I got here. Then I was in such a state Candy got the full story,' Gina admitted shyly. 'She's very nice, really, you know.'

He raised his eyebrows but didn't comment on that. What he did say was, 'Are you free tomorrow to go hunting for an engagement ring? We'll buy the wedding rings at the same time.'

She had to make sure. In spite of all he had said, the last year or so had taken its toll, and this had happened so quickly her head was still spinning. 'You don't have to do that,' she said slowly, her fingers playing with one of the buttons on his shirt. 'It would perhaps be more sensible to wait and see how you feel in a month or two.'

'In a month or two I'm hoping you might be carrying my child in there,' he said very softly, touching her belly.

Shocked, she raised her eyes to his and saw all the reassurance she'd ever need shining there.

'I love you, Gina. I'll love you for ever. I want to fill our house with love so it spills over onto our children and grandchildren, and their children. I want it all, OK? Cats, dogs, roses round the door, and you in my arms every night.'

She gulped, telling herself she couldn't cry, not when everything was so wonderful, but as a tear caught on her eyelashes she said brokenly, 'I've been so miserable without you.'

'And I without you. When you left the world became grey, you know?'

She nodded, joy, like warm honey, spreading throughout her body and healing all the hurt and pain.

'I'd look at the sunset and all I could think of was you. Were you looking at the same night sky? The knowledge that you were somewhere living, breathing, laughing, sleeping without me, was torture. All around the world was going on the same, and yet I was dying inside.'

She reached up and touched his face. 'I know.'

'Stay with me like this tonight?' he asked softly. 'I can't bear to let you out of my arms.'

She nodded. 'Can I change?' She wanted to wipe off the heavy eye make-up and brush out her hair, to feel herself again.

A smile curved his lips. 'Be quick.'

She was quick, slipping into her silk pyjamas and robe before she came back to him. Her heart jumped as she saw him, his legs stretched out and his head lying against the back of the sofa, eyes shut. He was so big and dark and handsome, so sexy. She couldn't believe he wanted her. But he did. Her heart told her so, even if logic was against it.

In the moment before he opened his eyes and held out his arms, she saw she wasn't the only one who was thinner. There was a raw leanness to the big frame that hadn't been there before. It melted her heart, but then everything about him melted her heart.

They talked and kissed, dozed and embraced the night away, and when Candy returned to the flat at first light she found them wrapped in each other's arms. She stood in the entrance to the sitting room, a big grin on her face as she took in Gina's shining face. 'Congratulations are in order, I take it?' she said drily.

Gina nodded. 'We're looking for an engagement ring today.'

Candy glanced at Harry, her brown eyes slightly mocking. 'You might be a late bloomer, but when you cotton on there's no stopping you, is there?' she drawled.

'You bet.' Harry's eyes had narrowed and his smile was controlled. 'And you'd better start looking for another flat-mate this week, because by this time next Saturday Gina will be Mrs Breedon.'

'No problem.'

'I'll cover her rent and any expenses until you get someone, of course.'

'You don't have to do that.'

'Yes, I do.' His smile took a wry twist. 'Without you, we might have gone on for months with our wires crossed.'

'Only months?' Candy queried, tilting her head.

He shrugged. 'I wouldn't have given up, however long it took.'

Candy surveyed him for a long moment. 'No, I don't think you would,' she said thoughtfully. 'From a bad start, I think I might get to like you after all, Gina's Harry.'

'Likewise.'

They were married by special licence within ten days, a quiet wedding with just immediate family in attendance. Harry had promised all their friends a big party when they were back from honeymoon.

Gina looked beautiful in her white dress, a silk crêpe frock which fell gracefully to the hips before flaring out in a plethora of Monroe-esque sunray pleats. And Harry looked very dashing in a grey suit with a white-and-gold waistcoat and white shirt and tie.

Everyone had a magical day, thoroughly enjoying the magnificent wedding lunch Mrs Rothman and one of her friends had had waiting for them when they returned to the cottage after the service. Gina didn't think she had ever been so happy.

Harry's parents were taking care of the dogs until Gina and Harry were back from their honeymoon in Italy, and so once everyone had left later that evening Gina and Harry were alone in their own home. Gina had expressly wanted it that way, refusing to go to a hotel or straight on honeymoon. Since Harry had proposed, she'd dreamt of waking up in his arms after a night of making love in their thatched cottage, the sun streaming through the windows, and wood pigeons cooing in the trees in the garden. Which was exactly what happened.

When she opened her eyes the room was bathed in sunlight,

the curtains moving gently in the warm breeze from the open window. Harry was still asleep, one hairy arm lying possessively over her stomach, and his long eyelashes resting on the tanned skin of his face. She lay, drinking in every curve and hollow of his face, before her eyes moved over the strong tanned throat and muscled chest.

This was her *husband*. She lifted her left hand and looked at the exquisite diamond engagement-ring and white-gold band nestling beside it. She had the right to lie beside him every night in this huge bed, to wake up next to him, to touch and caress him. It was more than she had ever hoped for. *He* was more than she had dared to hope for.

And their wedding night… She closed her eyes for a moment, a delicious thrill trickling over her whole body.

She had been embarrassed to admit she hadn't slept with a man before him, but she needn't have been. He had taken it as a gift, a precious gift—he'd told her so. And then he had set out to initiate her into all she had been missing.

She had expected the first time to be… She shook her head. She didn't know, not really, but certainly not the night of passion that had ensued. He had spent hours showing her how much he loved her, and he had been so tender and patient, touching and tasting her, bringing her to the brink of fulfillment time and time again, before he had finally taken her. And even then he had restrained his own need and desire until she'd been as ready as him, prolonging the exquisite pleasure his possession had caused, until there'd been no room for anything but the delicious quest for the next peak of delectation.

Her body felt sensuously alive, the core of her throbbing with a pleasurable ache, and every part of her tingling with the knowledge she was loved. Whatever happened now, whatever life threw at them, they would weather it together. There were no promises the sky would always be blue as it was today, how could there be? Life was a series of milestones, it was that way for everyone. But not everyone had love as the anchor of their soul.

She was lucky. She was so, *so* lucky.

'Good morning, Mrs Breedon.'

His deep smoky voice brought her out of her thoughts, and she focused on his face. He was smiling. She smiled back, turning into the curve of him as she whispered, 'Good morning, Mr Breedon.'

'Every day for the rest of our lives we can say that.' His voice reflected the wonder in her own heart.

'I know.' Her eyes brimming with love, she murmured huskily, 'And every night we can lie in each other's arms and make love.'

'Well, actually…' He ran his hands over her body, bringing her hips into his where she felt his body's response of her nakedness. 'We can do that in the morning too.'

She giggled, moving her hips in a sinuous and blatant invitation as she whispered, 'Are you sure it's allowed?'

'Oh yes,' he said, his breath catching in his throat on a groan. 'In fact, it's written into the marriage document. Didn't you know?'

She shook her head, sliding her hands down and caressing his erection so he nearly shot out of his skin. 'But I approve,' she whispered against his mouth. 'We'll have to make sure we adhere to that, if it's official.'

And they did.

Undressed
BY THE BOSS

From sensible suits...into satin sheets!

Even if at times work is rather boring, there is one
person making the office a whole lot more interesting:
the boss! He's in control, he knows what he wants and
he's going to get it! He's tall, handsome, breathtakingly
attractive. And there's one outcome that's never in
doubt—the heroines of these electrifying, supersexy
stories will be undressed by the boss!

*A brand-new miniseries available only from
Harlequin Presents!*

Available in August:

TAKEN BY THE
MAVERICK MILLIONAIRE

by Anna Cleary

Book # 2754

In September, don't miss another breathtaking boss in

THE TYCOON'S VERY
PERSONAL ASSISTANT

by Heidi Rice

www.eHarlequin.com

HPI2754

HIRED: THE SHEIKH'S SECRETARY MISTRESS

Sheikh Amir has a convenient wife lined up by his
family. His requirements: no love, but plenty of heat in
the bedroom! But he's becoming quite inconveniently
attracted to his sensible secretary...and Amir wants to
promote her—into his bed!

A man driven by desire—who will he make his bride?

*Don't miss the next sizzling installment
of fan favorite*

Lucy Monroe's

Royal Brides series

HIRED: THE SHEIKH'S SECRETARY MISTRESS
Book #2747

On sale August 2008.

They seek passion—at any price!

A sizzling trilogy by

Carole Mortimer

Two brothers and their cousin are all of
Sicilian birth—and all have revenge in mind
and romance in their destinies!

In July you read Cesare's story in

THE SICILIAN'S RUTHLESS MARRIAGE REVENGE

In August, read Wolf's story in

AT THE SICILIAN COUNT'S COMMAND

Book #2750

Count Wolf Gambrelli annoyed Angelica—and aroused her!
He'd been appointed her live-in protector, and it was clear that
Wolf also desired Angelica, and he'd stop at nothing to bed her.

Don't miss Luc's story in

THE SICILIAN'S INNOCENT MISTRESS

Available September!

www.eHarlequin.com

HP12750

REQUEST YOUR FREE BOOKS!

2 FREE NOVELS PLUS 2 FREE GIFTS!

PASSION GUARANTEED SEDUCTION

YES! Please send me 2 FREE Harlequin Presents® novels and my 2 FREE gifts (gifts are worth about $10). After receiving them, if I don't wish to receive any more books, I can return the shipping statement marked "cancel". If I don't cancel, I will receive 6 brand-new novels every month and be billed just $4.05 per book in the U.S. or $4.74 per book in Canada, plus 25¢ shipping and handling per book and applicable taxes, if any*. That's a savings of close to 15% off the cover price! I understand that accepting the 2 free books and gifts places me under no obligation to buy anything. I can always return a shipment and cancel at any time. Even if I never buy another book, the two free books and gifts are mine to keep forever.

106 HDN ERRW 306 HDN ERRL

Name _____ (PLEASE PRINT)

Address _____ Apt. #

City _____ State/Prov. _____ Zip/Postal Code

Signature (if under 18, a parent or guardian must sign)

Mail to the Harlequin Reader Service:
IN U.S.A.: P.O. Box 1867, Buffalo, NY 14240-1867
IN CANADA: P.O. Box 609, Fort Erie, Ontario L2A 5X3

Not valid to current subscribers of Harlequin Presents books.

**Want to try two free books from another line?
Call 1-800-873-8635 or visit www.morefreebooks.com.**

* Terms and prices subject to change without notice. N.Y. residents add applicable sales tax. Canadian residents will be charged applicable provincial taxes and GST. Offer not valid in Quebec. This offer is limited to one order per household. All orders subject to approval. Credit or debit balances in a customer's account(s) may be offset by any other outstanding balance owed by or to the customer. Please allow 4 to 6 weeks for delivery. Offer available while quantities last.

Your Privacy: Harlequin Books is committed to protecting your privacy. Our Privacy Policy is available online at www.eHarlequin.com or upon request from the Reader Service. From time to time we make our lists of customers available to reputable third parties who may have a product or service of interest to you. If you would prefer we not share your name and address, please check here. ☐

HP08R

I ♥ HARLEQUIN *Presents*

BROUGHT TO YOU BY FANS OF HARLEQUIN PRESENTS.

> We are its editors and authors and biggest fans—and we'd love to hear from YOU!

Subscribe today to our online blog at www.iheartpresents.com

EXTRA

BOUGHT FOR HER BABY

Taken for her body…and her baby!

These men always get what they want—
and the women who produce their heirs
will be their brides!

**Look out for all our exciting books
in August:**

#17 THE MARCIANO LOVE-CHILD
by MELANIE MILBURNE

**#18 DESERT KING,
PREGNANT MISTRESS**
by SUSAN STEPHENS

**#19 THE ITALIAN'S
PREGNANCY PROPOSAL**
by MAGGIE COX

#20 BLACKMAILED FOR HER BABY
by ELIZABETH POWER

Harlequin Presents® EXTRA delivers popular themed
collections every month featuring four new titles.